GHOST LIGHT *Killer*

DAHLIA DONOVAN

HOT TREE PUBLISHING

For information, contact the publisher, Hot Tree Publishing.

www.hottreepublishing.com

Editing: Hot Tree Editing

Cover Designer: BooksSmith Design

E-book ISBN: 978-1-922359-76-6

Paperback ISBN: 978-1-922359-77-3

ONE

OSIAN

"This is Oz and D with Osian's and Danny's London Crime Podcast. We've got a real treat for everyone. We'll be talking all things crime and ghostly in the West End, getting a tour of a few theatres with up close and personal tales of close encounters of the terrifying kind." Osian paused the recording, satisfied with the brief intro to their next episode. He grinned over at his boyfriend, who rolled his eyes. "What? It's perfect."

"Still not sure about Oz and D," Dannel teased. "Plus, it took you five takes to say a paragraph."

"Rude and unnecessary."

"Is that non-autistic talk for accurate and truthful?" Dannel grinned at him. "What happened to 'it'll only take me a minute to record the intro'?"

"Ian will be fashionably late as per usual." Osian leaned across the table to brush a kiss against Dannel's lips. "It's boiling in here."

"It's almost summer. I imagine we're going to have the hottest on record." Dannel rubbed his fingers across his shortened hair. They'd both gone for shorter cuts with the unseasonably warm weather. May had been ten degrees above average, which didn't bode well for July or August. "Ian will be here soon."

"In a swirl of his scarf." Osian watched Dannel continue to rub his head. Neither of them was used to the shorter length yet; Dannel, in particular, found it slightly uncomfortable at times.

They loved their eldest neighbour. Ian Barrett had fully recovered from his brush with poison the previous month—one meant for Osian. The seventy-six-year-old was a retired actor/director who consulted with a small local theatre troupe. Ian was finalising the details on a musical after spending over a year working on it. Osian and Dannel had been invited to investigate a supposed ghost haunting the show.

Just a few weeks back, they'd faced down a flesh-and-blood danger. A ghost didn't seem too threatening. Osian hadn't completely recovered from his brush with death.

A killer had set their eyes on Osian after one of his patients passed away while he'd worked as a paramedic. His last call-out had been a horrific traffic incident where several people had died despite their best efforts. Two relatives had decided he and the other emergency responders should pay —with their own lives.

Life had changed drastically in the short time since the killer had been captured—aside from the haircuts. Osian had returned to therapy to combat the worsening of his post-traumatic stress. The podcast, Dannel, and their family had helped pull him through.

Now a retired firefighter at the young age of thirty, Dannel had tried a volunteer position. He'd been eaten up with guilt at not going out when emergencies came in and decided to quit. His time now went to building a cosplay fabrication business, something they both worked on together, as always. They'd been joined at the hip from infancy, growing up next door to each other. From best friends to boyfriends, Osian had never looked at anyone else. Ever.

"Are you pulling out your Constantine costume?"

Osian was yanked from his thoughts by Dannel holding up a bottle of blond hair dye. "It's easiest."

Aside from his dark brown hair, Osian bore a striking resemblance to the actor who'd portrayed the character—Matt Ryan. Close enough he was practically his doppelganger aside from his bright blue eyes. His Constantine costume got used frequently.

"How about you? Washington from *Hamilton*?" Osian had a particular fondness for seeing his boyfriend in the tight breeches from the musical.

Dannel paused in helping him pack up their recording equipment to glare at him. "Get your mind out of the gutter. I'm not wearing breeches. Thought I might go as Maurice Moss from *The IT Crowd*, even though I've trimmed my afro down."

"You'll be glad when summer hits." Osian thought the Moss costume would go down a treat. Dannel was a buffer, taller version of Richard Ayoade, after all.

"Did you miss the part where I'm already boiling?" Dannel grabbed a card from the table to fan himself. "It's hot. Inside voice?"

"Definitely," Osian assured him.

As an autistic, Dannel often struggled to modulate his voice. He'd whisper or shout. Osian had gotten used to helping him find an even tone whenever Dannel asked.

"Bonjour, my darlings," a cheerful voice called out before their doorbell rang. "I shall await you downstairs."

Shooting a bemused glance at Dannel, Osian grabbed his wallet and phone. He tossed Dannel's iPhone over to him. They caught up to Ian on the stairs; he waved the edge of his colourful, thin scarf at them.

"It isn't often two dashing gentlemen escort me to the theatre." Ian slipped his lanky arm through Osian's. He waited for a nod of permission from Dannel before repeating his action on the other side. "You'll do wonders for my reputation. They'll wonder how I keep up with you both."

"Ian." Osian dodged to the right to avoid walking straight into a woman fighting with her umbrella.

"Are we walking too quickly?" Dannel slowed his pace.

"Not that kind of keeping up," Osian explained.

"Ah. In bed?" Dannel occasionally struggled with innuendo or any conversation that assumed the listener grasped subtext between the words. He tended to take things literally. "In bed? With Ian?"

"It will feed my dreams for days." Ian ignored both of their groans. "Shall we stop for a coffee?"

Osian decided the change of subject was for the best. "There's a café across from your theatre. How are your rehearsals going?"

"You'd make a lovely musical." Ian sidestepped the question.

"What?" Osian didn't know how to respond to Ian's confident statement. "Me, specifically?"

"Star-crossed lovers. Osian Kincaid Garey, a former paramedic. Myron Dannel Ortea Junior, a former firefighter. And their handsome, wise neighbour, Ian Barrett." He smiled beatifically and patted Osian's arm. "My rehearsals are going splendidly. I don't even mind the ghost. It adds a certain something to the atmosphere."

"We're not the Ghostbusters," Dannel commented.

"We did cosplay as Ghostbusters a few years ago." Osian ducked away when Dannel tried to reach around Ian to yank his shirt. "We did?"

"Not the point." Dannel bickered with him all the way to the coffee shop. Ian seemed entertained by both of them.

Given the morning crowd, Osian slipped into the café to grab coffees for the three of them. He was excited. They hadn't had any guests on their podcast aside from Detective Inspector Khan; this might prove to be an exciting new direction for them.

The podcast had grown significantly from where it started. Osian had never imagined anyone aside from friends and family listening in, but their audience continued to grow each week.

Three coffees and a box full of assorted mini scones later, Osian carried his purchases outside. Dannel immediately grabbed the scones from him. Typical. They went up the street, around a corner, and found themselves standing in front of the iconic Evelyn Lavelle, one of the smaller West End theatres. It was named for the legendary Edwardian actress Evelyn Lavelle, who'd been one of the most photographed women of the time. A portrait of her by the artist of the time hung backstage in the theatre. Her beautiful voice and visage were said to haunt the dressing rooms.

The theatre was a small space, with two levels of seating in a historic building from the early 1900s. Osian had always loved the Evelyn Lavelle. With beautiful, brilliant acoustics, the sound carried in a way modern auditoriums could only pretend to replicate.

Of all the theatres they'd been to, the Evelyn Lavelle certainly felt as though it might be haunted. It had been well cared for and occasionally restored to perfection over the years. He often wondered if actors and actresses from the golden age of the twenties haunted the stage.

"Are we ready?" Ian sipped his coffee before adjusting his scarf carefully around his neck. He paused when a hideous scream came from inside the theatre. "Oh dear, sounds as though the ghost has struck again."

Osian exchanged a worried glance with Dannel. "Maybe we should head inside?"

Ian led them into the theatre. They found a crowd gathered backstage in front of a door. "What's going on? Let me through."

Osian stayed close behind Ian. He managed to peer between the gawkers and could only stare in shock. "Archie?"

"Oz?" Archie was kneeling on the floor, almost keening in grief, bent over a grey-haired woman prone on the ground. He leaned back to turn tear-filled eyes toward Osian. "Oz. Help her. Please?"

"Someone call 999." Osian shoved his way

through the gathered actors and stagehands. He dropped to his knees beside Archie, trying to assess the situation. "Hurry. Someone call 999. There's not much time."

Damn it all.

It's already too late.

"I've got it." Ian fumbled in his pocket for his phone. "Everyone make room. He's a paramedic."

Former paramedic.

We should've stayed at home.

"Does anyone know who she is?" Osian tried to delicately assess the health of the woman on the floor without moving her. He couldn't see her face. His attention was focused on the scissors plunged into her back. "Archie?"

"My mum."

And our morning was going so well.

TWO

DANNEL

"Not you two again." Detective Inspector Haider Khan had pushed through the throng of onlookers, coming to a halt when he spotted Dannel and Osian. He pinched the bridge of his nose for several seconds. "Why am I not surprised?"

"We've got witnesses. It wasn't us," Dannel insisted immediately. "Definitely not us."

"Inside voice." Osian bent forward to whisper.

"Sorry." Dannel grabbed Osian's hand. "We were *definitely* not in the room where it happened."

Haider narrowed his eyes on them when Osian muffled his snort of amusement against Dannel's arm. "Small mercies, I suppose."

Surveying the room and the crowded hallway, the detective inspector waved over the constables who'd come with him. He dispatched them to herd the witnesses out into the auditorium. His partner, Detective Inspector Powell, joined him; her eyes widened when she caught sight of Dannel and Osian.

Dannel didn't want to risk unnecessary attention. He'd seen before how that almost led to Osian's arrest. "We'll join the other witnesses."

"Not so fast." Haider glanced around the room. Archie still stood in the far corner, pale and shaking, watching the paramedics finish up and step aside for the coroner. "While DI Powell speaks with your friend, why don't we move down the hall and you two tell me what happened?"

After their close encounters with the police the previous month, Dannel didn't envy Archie the sudden and full attention of Detective Inspector Powell. *Should we call someone?* Wayne Dankworth had been their solicitor and happened to be dating Dannel's younger brother, Roland.

Does dating your best friend run in our family? Maybe not. Myron certainly wasn't Mum's best friend. Or perhaps he was in the beginning, and I don't remember?

Is Mum right about my being unfairly harsh and not understanding what happened between them?

"Dannel?"

He blinked a few times when Osian waved his hand in front of him. "What?"

"Dead body. Detective. Questions."

Right. Focus. Family confusion after we deal with another murder. I hope this isn't going to be a trend.

"Are you okay?" Haider waited until they both nodded before pulling his notebook and pen out. He flipped through the pages to a fresh page. "Did you know the deceased?"

"Yes."

"No." Osian glanced over at Dannel. "Well, technically yes. Define 'know.'"

"Ossie." Dannel prodded Osian in the side. They might've become friendly with the detective inspector but now wasn't the time for jokes. "She's our friend Archie's mum. She worked here at the theatre. We were supposed to chat with her about the ghost. And maybe a few West End murder mystery legends for our podcast. We didn't know Archie would be here."

"By no, I meant we didn't know who was deceased at the time." Osian shrugged.

Haider blinked at Dannel and ignored Osian, obviously surprised at the unexpected and rapid flow of words. "And Archie is?"

"Her son?" Dannel thought they'd already

covered that piece of information. "Ossie knows him better. They worked together when they were both paramedics."

"We both quit after the London wreck." Osian leaned into Dannel. He still hated talking about the horrific accident that had led to his leaving his beloved career with the ambulance service. "Archie. Archie Dennis. He chose to travel the world, something about finding himself and living life to the fullest. Gemma knew him best."

Poor Gemma. A paramedic friend who'd been murdered a month prior. The first shot across the bow by the murderers who'd been after Osian. Dannel was relieved they'd never have to worry about them again.

The weeks following Gemma's death had been strange. Grief. Dannel didn't understand the grieving process; he was sad about her death, but life moved on as it always did. He'd tried to be patient with Osian, who'd been genuinely devastated.

His brother, Roland, had explained that grief hit everyone differently. Dannel had been sad over Gemma's passing. The emotion had flowed over him like a calm breeze, where Osian seemed to be battered by gale-force winds. Four weeks on, Osian had begun to return to normal.

"And his mother?" Haider pulled Dannel out of his thoughts. "What was their relationship like?"

"Good?" Dannel shrugged. He hadn't known Mrs Dennis really well. "He did say she didn't approve of his new boyfriend."

"New boyfriend?" Osian interrupted whatever Detective Inspector Khan had been about to say. "Since when?"

"You missed the last coalition meeting." Dannel tended not to gossip about relationship stuff. Not because he was above it, but he usually forgot to tell Osian. "Freya and Abra mentioned it."

"How do you forget to tell me about Archie's new boyfriend? I could've bugged him in my last message." Osian pouted. "Rude. What's his name?"

"No idea." Dannel hadn't been interested.

"Coalition?" Haider interrupted their conversation.

"The LGBTQ+ First Responder Coalition. A support group for former and current paramedics, police officers, and firefighters. We all started it three or four years ago. Abra and Evie currently run the organisation together." Osian and Dannel were both inordinately proud of having helped create the coalition. It had snowballed into a more extensive gathering than they ever imagined, offering encouragement, counselling, or simply a mutual understanding. "Archie was one of the original founding members. We're all quite close."

"Let's get back to today." Haider tried to pull them back to Mrs Dennis. "Did either of you touch the body?"

"I attempted resuscitation," Osian admitted.

"Of course, it had to be you." Haider pinched the bridge of his nose. "I need to speak with the other witnesses. Don't go anywhere yet, will you? I might have more questions."

"Why don't we wait in my dressing room?" Ian came over once Haider moved on and led them through narrow hallways and down a flight of stairs. He paused in front of a white door covered with cheerful notes from friends and admirers. "In we go."

Huddling in one corner of the room, Dannel and Osian had a moment to regroup. They tried to ignore the wildly gesturing Ian while he hyperventilated into his iPhone. The police were still questioning their way through the cast and crew.

"Could Archie have murdered his mum?"

Dannel kept his voice low, bending his head closer to Osian. "With scissors?"

"Bit like Ron Weasley killing Mrs Weasley, isn't it?"

"Less ginger and probably less freckled, but yes." Dannel tried to picture Archie in a rage but couldn't. "Actually, no, nothing like it. Bad analogy."

"Fair enough. Ruin my joy," Osian grumbled.

There were loads of words to describe Archie. Jovial. Wild, even down to his curly reddish-brown hair. Paramedic. Traveller. Loyal. Dannel would never have imagined a murderer being part of the list. He knew Osian didn't want to believe the worst of their friend either.

"Boys." Ian had finished his call; his sudden full attention on them made Dannel uneasy. "Can you believe this? First, a ghost. Then an actual murder?"

"Is your play cancelled?"

"Cancelled? A murder might just draw in even more of a crowd than my humble appearance." Ian brandished his phone in their direction. "You boys simply must solve this case for me."

"Ian." Dannel nudged Osian when he began to snicker. "We're not detectives."

"Aren't you?" Ian adjusted the scarf around his neck. "You've already solved one murder mystery. Why stop there? Wouldn't it make your podcast about the West End more exciting?"

"Not sure we solved anything so much as we survived long enough for the police to do their jobs." Osian hopped up on the nearby dressing table. "Plus, the killers weren't trying overly hard not to get caught."

"How shall I go on if you won't investigate the murder of my dearest friend?" Ian swooned into his grand chair in the corner. He covered his eyes with one hand, peeking through his fingers at them. "Well?"

"Us investigating doesn't actually impact your ability to survive." Dannel glanced over at Osian when he nudged his leg. "What? Oh. Hyperbole. Not literal."

Osian squeezed Dannel's knee. "I doubt Haider will enjoy our unwanted interference."

"I will pay you in adoration and praise." Ian winked exaggeratedly at the both of them.

"Adoration and praise mean the same thing." Dannel tucked his hand into his pocket to pull out his earbuds. "I'm going to sit outside."

Leaving Ian and Osian to discuss the non-investigation, Dannel meandered up through the theatre until he made it outside. He plugged his earbuds in and upped the volume on his video game playlist. Sometimes the only thing that helped his mind settle was music.

Musical silence.

Four songs into his playlist, Dannel managed to relax his shoulders. He enjoyed being around people, to an extent. Being alone was better.

Not alone. With Osian. Music and Osian had always helped him.

Osian plopped down beside Dannel on the bench outside the theatre. "Haider said we can go. He knows where to find us. Not much point in trying to ask about the ghost or for a tour. Archie's still with the detectives."

"I can't see him killing anyone." Dannel had a clearer head after listening to the music. "Let alone his mum."

"Me either."

"Are we poking our nose in?" He leaned into Osian. "A little?"

"I sent Wayne a text. He's going to check in on Archie to see if he needs a solicitor." Osian tapped his phone in his pocket. "Better safe than sorry."

"Better safe than wrongfully accused of murder."

"So, we're definitely asking a few questions," Osian commented after a moment of silence. "For Archie."

"For Archie." Dannel figured they didn't need to mention their own curiosity and obsession with true crime.

"That's what friends are for."

"Solving the murder of their mum?" Dannel stared at him.

"Doesn't quite roll off the tongue." Osian glanced back at the theatre. "I wonder if we'll be able to chat with Archie."

"Why don't you wait? I'll head home." Dannel scratched at his palms, trying to alleviate the sensation of cooped up energy underneath his skin. "Need some…."

They were both silent for a few minutes. The rush of adrenaline had carried them through the moment of finding Archie's mum but had swiftly evaporated. Dannel dropped his face into his hands.

"Poor Archie." Dannel didn't quite know how to put into words. "I can't imagine losing my mum."

"I—" Osian cut himself off. He cleared his throat a few times. "We shouldn't think about it."

"Maybe we should." Dannel decided to call his mum later to say hello. "Not sure I can sit still here."

"Go on then." Osian tapped the bench between them, knowing Dannel well enough not to touch him at the beginning of what they both recognised as a meltdown. "I'll bring home an early tea for us."

"Cake."

"When have I ever not bought cake?" Osian knocked his knuckles against the bench a second time. "Shoot me a text when you're ready for me to invade our space again."

THREE

OSIAN

"Now, who are you?" Osian watched a well-dressed young woman dart into the theatre with her face shielded by a monstrosity of a hat. "Odd. Ian never mentioned any famous starlets in his beloved show."

"Osian." Detective Inspector Khan stepped through the front entrance and came to sit on the bench beside him. "Try not to play inspector."

"Would I do that?"

Haider turned his head slowly toward Osian, lifting his eyebrows up in obvious disbelief. "In the time I've gotten to know you and Dannel. Yes, yes, you would."

"Fair enough." Osian focused on the traffic

passing in front of them for several seconds. "She was dead before we entered the room."

"Yes."

Osian shoved his hands into his pockets, trying to keep from fidgeting incessantly. "The paramedic in me feels as if I should've been able to make a difference."

"That's not the paramedic in you, it's survivor's guilt." Haider had spoken at length with Osian on the subject of post-traumatic stress and dealing with losing patients. "Something most of us in the service do."

"I'll never be able to square not saving a life."

Haider breathed in and out deeply a few times. "This isn't a video game where a healer throws a resuscitation potion and everyone lives. Your best efforts never guarantee a patient's survival. And they can't. Shouldn't, really."

Osian couldn't argue with the detective inspector's logic, so he chose to stare blankly in silence at the traffic building in front of them.

"Have you considered hosting a paramedic hour on your podcast?" Haider broke the silence after a while. "Talking through everything might help you and others. You're not the only first responder struggling with burnout. It's a serious issue we're feeling across the services."

"Not sure my true crime podcast is the solution." Osian cringed at the idea. *Am I ready to delve into my years as a paramedic? Capable of dredging things up?* "I don't know."

"Start a second one." Haider held a hand up when Detective Inspector Powell whistled for him by the entrance. "Maybe focus on sharing your experiences with burnout and losing a patient. It may help you find some peace."

"Thank you, Obi-Khan." Osian grinned at the inspector, who rolled his eyes and heaved an exhausted sigh. "Can I chat with Archie, or are you holding him for questions?"

"Leave it alone, Osian." Haider squeezed his shoulder. "He'll probably call you when we're done with him."

So, that's a no, then.

Definite no.

Retrieving his phone from his pocket, Osian checked for a response from Wayne. *Nothing. What good is a solicitor friend if they don't respond to you immediately? Useless. Well, time for cake, since Archie's not going anywhere for the moment.*

With no message from Dannel either, Osian decided to pop by his best friend's, Abra Gidney, place. She'd finished her four-day shift and had the next few days off. He grabbed a couple coffees, almond croissants, and cinnamon buns. *Never too early for elevenses.*

Abra opened the door still in her oversized striped pyjamas. "Morning. Go away."

"You wound me, Abs. I even brought you croissants." Osian waved the bag in front of her. "Buongiorno."

"What?"

"Thought you were learning Italian to appease your ancestors."

"Sod off. I haven't had coffee yet. Also, I'm telling my nan you called her ancient."

"Ancestor. Not ancient. And shouldn't you call her your nonna?" Osian teased.

"I'll call you something."

"Do you want the coffee and croissant or not?" Osian chuckled when she grabbed him by the arm to drag him into her flat. "Wait. Are you wearing Freya's pyjamas? Thought you were over your ex?"

"I say this with all the love in the world. Shut up and give me the pastry." She swatted him lightly on the arm. "Why are you out and about this morning? I thought you were heading to the theatre."

"You've missed loads."

"We spent most of the night chatting while playing *Elder Scrolls* online. What could I possibly have missed in twelve hours?" Abra clutched at the coffee he'd handed to her, taking a long sip of the warm liquid. "Brilliant invention, coffee."

"Isn't it just?" Osian flopped down onto her slightly lumpy sofa. "We went to the theatre with Ian."

"Always a lively one."

"Less lively and more deadly, as it turns out." Osian shook his head and stared into his coffee.

"What?"

"We were starting our tour of the theatre when we found Archie." Osian paused for nothing more than dramatics and to annoy Abra, who huffed at him. "We discovered our dear friend bending over his mum's body."

"Oh my god." Abra set her cup down after almost dropping it. "Are you joking?"

"Not even a little bit." He leaned back against the cushions. "He can't have murdered his mum, can he?"

"Archie? Our Archie? The gentle giant of a paramedic?"

"He's been hiking around the world for ages."

Osian plucked a toasted almond off his croissant and tossed it into his mouth. "He might've changed."

"From cuddly healer to homicidal wanker?"

"I admit it's a stretch." Osian's instincts told him Archie hadn't murdered his mother. He'd been attempting to save her. "I'm sure the police will find the killer."

"Are you?"

He considered his brief brush with being mistaken for a murderer. "Fifty-fifty."

"You and Dannel could—"

"Not you as well." Osian cut her off. "Why does everyone suddenly think I'm Sherlock Holmes?"

"More Miss Marple."

"Oi." He threw one of the decorative pillows at her. "Rude."

"Accurate."

"Mostly rude. Though, imagine if I cosplayed as Miss Marple. How brilliant would that be?" Osian made a mental note to add it to his list of potential costumes for the year. "Detective Inspector Khan suggested I do a paramedics hour podcast. He thought it might help me process Gemma's loss and the trauma left behind from my work."

Abra pointedly kept her gaze focused on her croissant. "And?"

"What good would it do?"

"You're not the only first responder in London—or the world, for that matter—to deal with the consequences of daily trauma. We see so much in our jobs. Not everyone copes well. And we shouldn't be expected to bounce back as if we've done nothing more than dance among the tulips." Abra leaned forward in her chair, pointing her croissant chunk at him. "Why don't you and I work on this paramedic podcast together? We can bring in guest speakers. Have specific topics."

"Have you been narking to Haider?"

"Oz."

"Fine," he grumped.

Showing how long they'd known each other, Abra quickly changed the subject. They chatted for over an hour before Dannel texted him. Osian gave her a quick hug and headed out the door.

While always open to leaving Dannel to settle himself in peace, Osian worried. How could he not? He'd loved Dannel since before they'd been old enough to understand what romance, relationships, and love even were.

"Oz?" a familiar voice called out to him, halting his progress down the crowded pavement.

"Archie." Osian stepped to one side, allowing rushing people to go by. He waited for his old friend to catch up to him. "I see the police finished up with you."

"For now." Archie grabbed him roughly by the arms, a hint of desperation evident in his voice and eyes. "Can we go somewhere and talk?"

Osian had promised to bring home a takeaway from Ecco Pizza. Dannel likely wouldn't mind adding a jolly paramedic giant to the mix. "Why don't I text my man to see if he's okay with extra company? You can tell us both what happened, save me from having to repeat the tale."

"I didn't hurt my mum," he blurted loudly enough that a passing couple almost tripped over their feet.

Osian wanted to laugh at the alarmed glances from the couple. None of this was funny. "Well, I'm sure those pensioners are pleased to hear you didn't."

"Oz." Archie scrubbed his hands across his face. "I'm serious."

"Yeah, I know, mate. I know. Maybe we should take this somewhere less public, though?" Osian wrapped an arm around Archie's shoulders. "Come on. Let's grab a pizza or four and head home."

After picking up two pizzas and several pulled pork burritos, they made their way home. Archie stared morosely at the box in his arms. Osian decided to leave him to his thoughts until they reached the flat.

Aside from the sounds of music and eating, the flat was filled with an uneasy lack of conversation. Dannel focused on his pizza, Archie danced around the conversation he wanted to have, and Osian simply waited for him to get comfortable.

Dannel finished up his last slice, wiped his fingers off, and turned to Archie. Osian held his breath, knowing a more direct approach was all but guaranteed. "Did you kill your mum?"

"Dannel." Osian covered his face with his hands to hopefully hide his grin.

Dannel waved off his reproach. "We might as well get the conversation out on the table. All this dancing around will give me indigestion. He asked for our help."

"It's a fair question." Archie recovered from his initial shock well. "I didn't hurt her. We did argue the first week I was home, I told the inspector. I loved my mum; everyone did. Well, almost."

"Argued?" Osian zeroed in on one of the critical parts of the admission. "About what? And who didn't she get along with?"

"My boyfriend." Archie smiled somewhat bitterly. "Niall Bishop. We met on one of my last hikes through Kathmandu. He travelled with me for months afterwards and agreed to come home with me when I decided to visit mum. Not two days after, she's telling me to break up with him."

"Why?" Dannel voiced the question on Osian's mind.

Birdie Dennis, for all her faults, had seemed to be a loving and accepting mother. She'd happily welcomed all of them into her house. Osian had enjoyed her slightly boisterous and larger than life personality.

"She claims he cheated." Archie shook his head, wiping a stray tear from his eye. "Claimed. She claimed to have seen him snogging some bloke outside the theatre."

Osian glanced over at Dannel, who shifted uneasily on the couch beside him. He caught the slight gesture of his hand, a sign he wanted him to say something. "We're sorry for your loss, mate. It can't be easy to be dealing with all of this."

But did your boyfriend murder your mum?

Or did you?

Nope, I definitely can't fling questions like that at him.

"I keep seeing those bloody scissors." Archie tossed his burrito haphazardly onto the plate. He covered his mouth, then darted out of the living room toward the nearest bathroom.

"You're cleaning up after him." Dannel grimaced.

"Brilliant." Osian lounged against him, resting his head on Dannel's shoulder while they waited for his return. Archie trudged back in several minutes later. "You all right?"

"You have to help me clear my name," Archie pleaded.

Osian twisted his head to smother a groan against Dannel's shoulder. *Haider's going to murder us himself if he catches us investigating.* "We'll do our best."

FOUR

DANNEL

TWO DAYS AFTER ARCHIE HAD PLEADED FOR THEIR help, Dannel found himself stressing over what to wear to a funeral. Osian had gone to help their friend with the details. Evie had come over to help.

In truth, today wasn't the funeral. Ian had thrown together a memorial of sorts. It was being held in an old church.

Evie Smith lived a floor up from their flat. His uncle, who owned and rented out the homes, had cut her quite a deal. It helped that her family came from the same neighbourhood in Jamaica as his dad and uncle; they considered themselves to practically be cousins.

Evie had become his closest friend when they'd gone through firefighting training together. She was only somewhat successful helping with his clothing dilemma, draped across the edge of his bed and mocking his clothing choices. "Listen, I adore you, but you're making a mountain out of this. Wear a black T-shirt and jeans. You'll be fine."

"Evie."

She peered over the top of her green cat-eye glasses at him. "Dan."

He collapsed onto the pile of clothes on the floor. "People get weird around funerals."

"Nothing brings out the worst in people like funerals and weddings." Evie got to her feet and stepped over him toward the wardrobe. She pulled out one of his nicer polo shirts and a dark grey pair of trousers. "Here. Not jeans but comfortable none-theless."

"See. You can be helpful." Dannel rolled his eyes when she dropped the clothes over his head. He yanked the fabric away. "What time are we leaving?"

"As soon as you quit having a crisis about what you're wearing." She dug through his closet to find a non-trainer pair of shoes. "Besides, the longer you take, the more people will have shown up."

"Not comforting."

"Yes, but it'll be easier to mingle and observe

potential suspects." Evie gestured towards the door of the en-suite. "Your clothes won't magically change."

"Endlessly disappointed I can't go into my inventory and simply select a new set of gear." Dannel thought so many things in life would be easier if they worked the same as video games. "Can you imagine if we could change the colour on our outfits like in *Dragon Age*?"

"You just want a cheese wheel backpack."

"Have you seen the one I'm fabricating for a client?" Dannel had taken on a commission for a leather chest piece and a cheese wheel shield. One of their friends intended to cosplay as Alistair from the first *Dragon Age* game. "Osian's been helping me with airbrushing. You've no idea how hard it is to get a massive thing of cheddar the perfect shade."

"And now I want cheese."

"You know where the fridge is. Help yourself while I get dressed." Dannel ushered her out of the bedroom. He flopped back on the bed to catch his breath. "I can do this."

With Evie raiding the fridge for cheese, Dannel made himself get ready for the memorial service. He wasn't looking forward to the day. Crowds.

Loads of people. Overly emotional. None of those things appealed to him.

Making sure to pocket his earbuds, Dannel steeled himself for the coming ordeal. He'd seen grief as a firefighter. It was never easy for him to process or deal with others who were mourning.

They made the short walk from their building down the street, up another until they reached the small church. Dannel wasn't surprised to see the large number of people gathered both inside and out. Birdie Dennis had been a popular part of the West End theatre, working behind the scenes on so many shows.

"Did you see…." Evie trailed off in shock, gesturing not so subtly towards one of her favourite actresses. "I feel faint."

"Why?" Dannel decided he didn't want an explanation and pressed on inside to try to find Osian. He spotted his boyfriend chatting with Wayne. "Evie's hyperventilating over one of the guests."

"I should check in with my new client. You two stay out of trouble. Please?" Wayne patted them both on the shoulders. "I don't need to try to keep you out of jail again."

"See the woman in the massive hat?" Osian

leaned into Dannel, keeping his voice low. "No, don't look."

"You literally told me to. How can I manage to see her without looking?" Dannel grumbled. "Knobhead."

"Git."

"Will you two quit swearing? We're in a church." Olivia swooped by with a bundle of flowers in her arms. "Honestly. Who raised you?"

"Your mum." Osian dodged away from his sister. "What? She's my mother too."

Olivia Garey-Rees was Osian's baby sister by a mere three years. A teacher who'd married one of Dannel's firefighter friends, Drystan Rees, a cheerful Welshman, Olivia tended to behave more like the older sibling.

Maybe it came from her years of teaching, although Olivia had always looked after her older brother. Osian found it highly entertaining. He usually watched with a proud gaze as she bulldozed her way through any difficulties and whipped people into behaving.

For his part, Dannel adored her. He'd dealt with his own insufferable younger brother, Roland, growing up. Olivia had been an angel by comparison.

"What are you two arguing about anyway?" She shifted closer to them to move out of the way. Her attention went to Dannel. "Got your earbuds?"

Dannel patted his pocket. "Of course."

"The woman in the massive hat." Osian nodded across the room. "I spotted her at the theatre the other day. She attempted to sneak inside. Badly. Almost cartoonish in her inept ability at stealth."

"Are you investigating again?" Olivia folded her arms and frowned at them.

"Never."

"Of course we are," Dannel answered at the same time. He never saw the point of lying unnecessarily. Olivia always managed to see through them anyway. "Archie asked."

Olivia shook her head at them and then shoved the flowers into her brother's arms. "Well, you won't solve anything by hovering at the edge of the crowd. Take the bouquet up to the table. You can accidentally-on-purpose run into the hat woman and introduce yourself. Mistake her for some famed ingénue of the West End."

Osian watched his sister vanish into the throng. He grinned over the bouquet at Dannel. "I swear she came out of the womb organised and in charge."

"Yes, but her ideas are usually better than ours." Dannel could write multiple pages worth of their terrible plans over the years. "Remember when—"

"No." Osian cut him off, shaking the bouquet in his face. "We don't need to alphabetically list all of our many bad ideas over the years."

"Your."

"Our," he insisted. He leaned forward to brush his lips against Dannel's. "Come on. Let's see if we can charm the hat woman into spilling her secrets."

With his arm looped through Osian's, Dannel kept his gaze focused anywhere but on people's faces. He nodded absently whenever someone greeted them in passing. Somewhere in the distance, he heard Ian's voice.

What's he up to now?

"Get out."

Dannel froze at the abrupt shout that had disrupted the relative quiet of murmured conversations happening around them. "Did you hear Archie?"

"Let's hurry." Osian dragged him forward to where they found Archie confronting the young woman in the overly decorated hat.

"Get out." Archie's face had gone bright red; his eyes were filled with tears while he towered over her. "Did you come to steal something else?"

"I beg your pardon. Just as rude as your mother," she snapped.

"Get the bloody hell out! You thieving...." Archie struggled to maintain his composure.

As the drama unfolded in front of them, Ian slipped in between Osian and Dannel. He'd dressed impeccably for the occasion, a black and white silk scarf draped delicately across his neck.

"Ian."

"Darling." He drew them away from the argument. "Why don't we let someone else deal with the poor dears?"

"Who's the bint in the hat?" Dannel figured Ian had to know.

"Ah. Yes." Ian adjusted his scarf. "Philippa Lewis. Costume designer who worked under dear Birdie. She practically apprenticed the child. They had a falling out a month ago, which eventually led to her being let go this past week."

"Is this when I get to go 'dun, dun, dun'?" Osian winked at Dannel who sighed. "You can't tell me the plot didn't thicken on us."

Dannel chose to ignore the silliness of Osian. It

was a defence mechanism, helping him deal with the stress of a funeral. He knew this would be a painful reminder of Gemma's death. "I'm more interested in why Archie accused her of thieving. What did she steal?"

"Unsubstantiated rumours." Ian waved a hand dismissively. "I do wonder how young Archie learned about it. Birdie was never one to speak badly of someone unless absolutely necessary."

"Now you can say it." Dannel nudged his boyfriend.

"Dun, dun, dun."

"I also heard young Archie had a little tiff with his amour outside the church. His lover stormed off. I couldn't have written a more dramatic start to our memorial for Birdie." Ian took them both by the arm. "Why don't I introduce you both to some of the cast? They're all here for our beloved designer."

"We can—" Osian protested, only for Ian to cut him off.

"How can you possibly discover the dastardly murderer without meeting everyone while they're either in mourning or pretending to be so?" Ian carried them toward the first group of whispering theatre enthusiasts. "You'll do fine."

Fine might have been a stretch. Dannel was

ready to leave. He'd lost track of names and faces; they all blended in together.

"Let's go home." Osian grabbed Dannel by the edge of his sleeve, tugging him in the direction of the side exit. They snuck through a narrow hallway toward the door leading out into the alley behind the church. "Shh."

"I didn't say anything." Dannel frowned at the back of Osian's head.

"Shh." Osian pressed closer to the open door. "Archie's out here."

"Okay?"

"With his boyfriend."

"Okay?" Dannel wanted to go home. He didn't want to see anyone, particularly Archie and Niall. "They're not snogging, are they?"

"Arguing. Damn. They went around the corner." Osian stood up straight and pulled the door open the rest of the way. "I could've sworn Archie said something about his mum."

"We shouldn't jump to conclusions about who might've murdered Birdie Dennis."

"True. We've got the police for that." Osian still held a grudge over being almost arrested for murdering one of his closest friends. "Well, maybe not Haider."

FIVE
OSIAN

"Cold pizza. Coffee shakes from Shake Shack. Thick, fluffy blankets. The Hamilton cast album." Osian ticked off the items on his "help Dannel relax" list. "Lights as dim as I can make them. Phones on vibrate. And a note on the door telling people not to knock unless the building is on fire."

"Ossie." Dannel always protested when Osian went out of his way to help on bad days. "We're supposed to be finishing up the podcast."

"We can't waste all the effort I went to in order for us to be lazy all afternoon." Osian flopped onto the sofa beside Dannel. He stretched his arm out to grab his shake. "The podcast can wait. Would you rather play the new *Uncharted*?"

"Pressing buttons takes more effort than I can

muster." Dannel selected one of the leftover slices of pizza. "Perfect temperature."

For most people, warmth offered comfort. Osian knew Dannel tended to crave cold food, pizza and shakes specifically, after a meltdown or any stressful event. Fast food and musicals weren't the worst coping mechanism in the world.

They ignored the footsteps and voices on the stairs. They were almost through the first act when a note slid under the door. Osian trudged over to retrieve it.

He held the paper up to show Dannel. "Adelle and Stanley bought slices of raspberry coconut loaf cake from Phoebe's."

Phoebe's Patisserie had opened up in an empty space near the park down the street from their building. Osian tried not to think about how much of her loaf cake they'd consumed in the past week. Adelle and Stanley regularly brought back treats after walking their dog; he wondered if they considered the two younger men to be their surrogate kids.

Osian cracked the door open, staring down to find a brown paper bag on the floor. "Thank you, kind cake faeries."

"Enjoy your evening, boys," Adelle called up to him.

"Cake." Osian locked the door behind him and carried the cake over to the sofa. "Now?"

"Coffee and cake do go nicely." Dannel lifted up his shake. "What do you think about Philippa Lewis?"

"Trying to be far more mysterious than she actually is." Osian had a feeling there was more to her firing. "Archie's reaction to her was interesting. It's a pity the theatre doesn't have CCTV cameras inside the building. I'd love to know if they had any sort of confrontation after she snuck inside."

The other pity was that the police wouldn't be able to determine who'd gone into the room. Archie had been found at the scene, but a video would've proven when. Then again, Osian had first-hand knowledge of how being found with a murder victim didn't necessarily prove guilt or innocence.

"Right." Dannel sat up, reaching over to turn down the music. He grabbed the last slice of cake and shoved it into his mouth before Osian could get the bag. "Why don't we make a list of our suspects? Archie has to be on there."

"Though, isn't he expecting us to prove his innocence?" Osian scraped off the last smear of raspberry from the bag. "Archie, Niall—the new boyfriend—and the hat lady."

"What about the ghost?"

"This isn't a horror movie."

Dannel whacked him over the head with a cushion. "No, you pillock, whoever is behind the ghost. What if the murder was an escalation for whatever their grand scheme actually happened to be? You don't go to the effort of haunting a theatre production for the fun of it."

Archie, Niall, Philippa, and a ghost.

Did Sherlock Holmes have to deal with this sort of nonsense? Then again, we're more Scooby and Shaggy than Holmes and Watson. At least they had snacks.

Snacks are good.

"Ossie?"

Osian glanced up to find Dannel flicking him on the leg. "Sorry, thinking."

"About?"

"What if we had Wayne and Roland throw a dinner party for our cosplay group? We can claim it's a welcome home for Archie, who will bring his boyfriend." Osian wanted a chance to watch the new couple in a controlled but friendly environment. "You never know what we might discover."

"Ossie." Dannel didn't seem convinced. "Music and games?"

"I'm sure everyone will be thrilled to play West End trivia or any other kind of drinking game we can come up with." Osian stretched his arm out to reach for his phone. "I'll text Roly Poly."

"Don't call him that to his face." Dannel stared mournfully at the empty paper sack. "Did we finish the cake?"

"Yes, you did, in fact, finish the last of the cake." Osian grunted when Dannel shoved him off the sofa to the floor. "Oi. How is this my fault? You ate the last slice."

After sending a text to Wayne and Roland, Osian pulled himself back up onto the sofa. He grabbed his laptop. They needed to get their thoughts organised, and he had to finish editing the next podcast episode.

Dannel twisted around to lean his back against the side of the sofa. He draped his legs across Osian's lap, who rested the laptop on top of them. "What do we know about Niall and Philippa? Our two strangers. Well, to us, at least."

"Not a damned thing." Osian decided to see what the internet said about Philippa Lewis. "Check this out."

Dannel bent forward to get a glimpse of the screen. "Impressive website. What's she selling?"

"Her costuming abilities." Osian frowned at one of the outfits. "The only problem I see is that I know Birdie designed and created at least three of these. They were part of the workshop we did last year, remember?"

"I don't remember Ms Lewis."

"No." Osian wondered if Archie's mum had known her assistant was claiming her designs as her own. Or had Birdie stolen the work from Philippa? "Archie's not going to like some of the questions I have for him. Damn it. Why can't murderers just admit to their crimes immediately?"

"Said every detective inspector everywhere." Dannel shifted on the sofa to get more comfortable. "Do a Google search for ghosts in the west end."

"There are a million posts. We might want to be more specific."

Dannel grabbed another slice of pizza. "What about the Evelyn Lavelle specifically? And search in the last six months? Ian's been working at the theatre on his project for a little longer than that. We know how gossip travels in the community. Someone has to have talked about it."

And they had.

It didn't require much finessing to find results from his search. Several theatre employees, cast, and visitors to the Evelyn Lavelle had posted on social media about their experiences. Hearing voices, seeing strange lights, or merely having the lights flickering. One person had gotten locked in one of the dressing rooms.

"Which dressing room?"

"The one supposedly used by Evelyn Lavelle, according to theatre lore." Osian twisted his laptop around to show him one of the videos of lights flickering. "The one where she died."

"Just looks like someone's playing with the circuit breaker." Dannel tended to be highly suspicious of anything claiming to be paranormal. Osian had a more open mind. "Think Ian could get us backstage to poke around?"

"What about the ghost light?" Osian loved teasing Dannel about all things superstition. His literal way of thinking tended to pick apart anything paranormal. "Maybe it's the spirits of past actors."

Ghost lights.

There was a belief in the theatre community that the spirits of former performers lingered behind on stage. Superstition led to most companies leaving a light on to guide them. Or to appease them, depending on who one asked.

"Ossie." Dannel rubbed his fingers roughly across his head, glowering at Osian, who grinned unrepentantly. "Just because they leave a light on, doesn't mean ghosts are actually there."

The superstition of the ghost light had always intrigued Osian. He knew, practically speaking, it probably evolved for safety reasons, allowing people to walk through a darkened theatre without injuring themselves. It was unlikely spirits cursed productions if they weren't appeased.

It was like most verbal histories. Somewhere along the line, the light left on stage had transformed into something mystically mysterious. The theatre did enjoy such things, after all.

"Doesn't the Palace keep two seats for any ghosts who attend performances?" Osian had read up on a number of London theatre ghostly superstitions.

"I haven't a clue." Dannel had not read anything on the paranormal secrets of stage. "Why?"

"If we do have someone faking a ghostly apparition at the Evelyn Lavelle, maybe they're trying to draw attention to Ian's play?"

"Or drawing attention away from the murder?" Dannel countered.

"True. Why don't we visit the theatre in the morning? After we get this sodding podcast episode up— Wait, don't you have a cheese shield to finish?" Osian had forgotten about the outstanding commission. "Do you need a hand?"

They often worked together on the painting aspect of cosplay. Dannel was far more gifted with fabrication than he. Osian didn't even pretend to have any skills with manipulating fabric and leather.

He did, however, have the patience required to glue googly eyes to armour when needed, an odd cosplay hack that made him laugh every time. They'd spray painted the round plastic bits, trans-forming them into perfect little rivets.

"So, I'll head to the theatre tomorrow morning while you work on the Alistair shield. We can have lunch, then try to track down Ms Lewis." Osian had quite a few questions for the woman. "Maybe Ian can help us with where she might be."

"Or confuse the situation further."

"He wouldn't be Ian if a few dramatics weren't thrown into the situation." Osian adored their older neighbour. He knew, at times, Dannel struggled to deal with the high level of enthusiastic energy Ian had. "We should *definitely* avoid the detectives."

Haider's going to read us the riot act if he finds out we're investigating.

"You're scared of Haider."

"Obi-Khan might arrest me again."

"Pretty sure he didn't *actually* arrest you the first time." Dannel, of course, had to throw logic into the conversation. "We'll be fine."

SIX

DANNEL

THE DAY HAD NOT GONE TO PLAN BY ANY STRETCH of the imagination. Dannel had gotten five minutes to work on his commission. Osian had left early with Ian, walking to the theatre together; he'd taken an hour to focus his mind.

And then the doorbell had rung.

Dannel answered the door wearing his ratty T-shirt and ripped jeans. He wore them to paint since ruining them didn't matter. "Myron."

"Son." His father stood side by side with Chief Wilson, Dannel's former boss at the fire station. "Can we chat with you?"

No.

Is no appropriate?

No should be appropriate.

"I'm busy with cheese." Dannel held up the glue in his hand. "Did you bring any cake?"

"Cake?" Myron stared at the pot of glue.

Chief Wilson pulled a Tupperware container out from behind his back. "My Martha missed you at the station supper this past weekend. She always appreciates how quiet you are compared to the riot of the other rabble. Insisted I bring you some of her sticky toffee apple and ginger cake."

"Cake." Dannel eyed the container suspiciously. He sighed and stepped back, allowing them inside the flat. "I don't do drugs."

"What the hell?" Myron stumbled over the edge of the carpet, obviously surprised by Dannel's statement. "Drugs? Why do you think we're here?"

"This is an intervention, right?" Dannel had watched an American show on the telly all about them. They always seemed to start with family members confronting someone. "What are you two doing together?"

"I wanted to talk," Myron admitted uncomfortably. "Your mum suggested your former chief might work as a mediator. Our conversations always go off the rails."

"Mum?" Dannel stared down at the Tupperware container in his hands. He didn't want to deal with Myron even with the filter of Fire Chief Harry Wilson. "So, indigestion is guaranteed."

It didn't surprise Dannel that his mum had suggested they talk. She'd long wanted to repair the relationship between father and son. It was hard to reconcile when stubbornness and miscommunication had been their foundation.

Make tea.

People always make tea when guests come over in movies.

I'm not sharing the cake. Do I have to share it? It's mine.

"Tea?" Dannel didn't wait for a response. He went into the kitchen and filled the kettle. "Or coffee?"

"Why don't we sit down, son?" Myron motioned toward the kitchen table. "We can chat without tea."

I don't want to have this conversation.

As a kid, Dannel hadn't grasped how adults might grow apart or fall out of love. He'd seen his dad abandoning his mum, not two people deciding to be happy separate instead of miserable together. His relationship with Myron hadn't completely recovered.

And Myron's vocal distaste for Osian and his constant poking at Dannel to step outside of his comfort zone hadn't helped matters.

"Coffee's fine. I've a long evening at the station ahead of me." Chief Wilson helped break the silence. "Are you going to share the cake?"

Dannel grabbed a tin from the counter to set on the table. "Biscuits."

"I see where we rate."

Three coffees and a fair portion of the biscuits hadn't eased the tension in the room. Dannel had a pile of crumbled Bourbons in front of him. He'd yet to consume one.

Why doesn't he just get to the point? Why do non-autistics always have to dance around a subject? It's so much simpler to be direct.

"For someone anxious to talk to me, you've said sod all so far." Dannel had a feeling his voice had risen louder than he'd wanted based on the raised eyebrows from his old fire chief. He missed Osian. Why had they decided to ambush him when Osian was out? "What did you want?"

"I never know how to talk to you." Myron shoved his mug away from him.

"You just did." Dannel thought Myron had been relatively free in his ability to say what he wanted to his son. "A whole sentence. I heard you."

"Don't be a smart arse."

"I'm not." Dannel scraped the mountain of

crumbs into his coffee mug. "How do you not know how to talk when you're steadily chatting up a storm while I crush Bourbons onto the table?"

"I want us to have the father-son relationship we should've all along," Myron insisted.

Dannel moved away from the table over to the sink. He set the mug down and tried to gather his thoughts. "You're not sick, are you? Why push now? We've been making progress. Talking without me slamming the door in your face. Why the sudden need for an intervention or mediation or whatever you're calling this?"

"I'm not sick."

Dannel waited while Myron continued staring down at his coffee mug. "I'm not adept at reading between the things. Something you'd know if you'd ever bothered to listen to me instead of talking at me or over me. I can't have this conversation with you."

"Why don't we come back when your Osian is here?" Chief Wilson showed how much better he knew Dannel compared to his own father. "Enjoy the cake. We'll text you to set up a meeting. Probably wiser than showing up unexpected."

Probably?

Definitely.

Don't be rude. They're going to leave. Don't be rude. I can blast whatever cast album I want once they're gone.

Despite Myron's protest, Chief Wilson practically strong-armed the man out of the flat. Dannel closed the door behind them, locking it and resting his head against hardwood with a tired groan. *What the hell was even the point of their showing up?*

Nothing.

His drive to be productive vanished, Dannel grabbed a slice of cake and a bottle of beer from the fridge. *Why bother?* The rest of the commission could wait; his energy had evaporated on him.

Right.

This isn't helping me at all.

Time to go for a workout.

After changing into his running gear, Dannel slid his trainers on and shoved in his earbuds. He ran the few blocks over to his favourite gym, one frequented by many of the firefighters who he'd worked with.

Please don't talk to me.

Please don't talk to me.

Please don't talk to me.

The pleasant young lad staffing the front desk waved him through with a smile. Earbuds were the greatest invention for anyone wanting to avoid conversation and not seem anti-social. Dannel managed to vent his frustration at everything by pummelling a punching bag and running his angst out on the treadmill.

An hour and a half made a vast improvement in his mood. He returned home in a better frame of mind, ready to at least attempt to craft. Costumes weren't going to make themselves.

Next time, I'm not answering the sodding door unless it's a food delivery I've ordered.

"Abandoned. Thrown away in the prime of my youth. Why are you laughing?" Ian draped himself against the ticket counter in the theatre lobby. "You're leaving me alone."

Osian simply raised his eyebrows, watching Ian's dramatics. "You asked me to poke around backstage since the police are gone. So, I'm going to head back there now."

"But who will bask in the glow of my brilliance?" Ian chuckled when Osian shook his head. "You've no sense of the dramatic."

"And you've got too much of it." Osian left Ian to sputter indignantly, making his way down the narrow passage into the guts of the building. He heard an odd sound in the distance beyond the main dressing rooms. "Don't get distracted. One place at a time."

With no evidence of a ghost in the hallway, whether real or pretend, Osian continued on to Birdie's costume design sanctuary. Police tape ran across the frame. He eased the door open and ducked underneath it.

The scent of bleach hit him almost immediately. Someone had been cleaning. *I wonder if Haider's aware his crime scene has been compromised. Or did the police release the scene back to the theatre?*

I'll text him later, much later, when he can't ask me pointed questions about why I want to know.

Or I could ask Ian.

With his first cursory glance, Osian thought the room looked like any theatre designer's sewing space. Completed costumes and works-in-progress littered the room, some hanging from cloth hangers on multiple racks. For a stabbing, there was no blood spatter to be seen on the fabric.

Osian knelt beside one of the more glamorous gowns for the show. He spotted several green spots on the silk. "What are you?"

Is that ink?

Why is ink splattered on the costume? Birdie surely

would've noticed. She was nothing if not meticulous about her artistry.

Using his phone to snap a few photos, Osian continued on with his inspection. He tried not to touch anything. The police were probably finished but no need to leave his fingerprints all over the place.

He'd learnt his lesson in the past month or so. Though, not enough, obviously, to keep himself from playing detective. A slamming door jolted him out of his inspection of Birdie's desk.

"What the—" Osian spun around to find the door had been pulled shut. He wandered over and tested the handle, only to find it impossible to open. "I do *not* believe in ghosts."

Yanking with all his strength, Osian fell on the floor when the door swung open. He jumped to his feet, rushing into the empty hallway. *Nothing. What on earth?* A low, scratchy laugh in the distance sent shivers up his spine.

Right. No more investigating on my own. Just in case ghosts do exist.

Well, maybe a little investigating.

Osian crept down the passageway, peering around the corner and into the stairwell. *Someone's taking the mickey. There can't be an actual ghost, can there?*

Retracing his steps to Birdie's sewing room; Osian continued his inspection of her desk. The police had likely removed anything pertinent to the murder. He hoped.

Haider was a thorough detective.

"Now, you're interesting." Osian spotted bottles of ink lined along the wall at the back of the desk. "Blue, black, red. No green. And no giant arrow pointing to a clue with a flashing neon sign of the killer's name. Rude. And inconvenient."

After making sure to seal the door without dislodging the caution tape, Osian went out into the theatre where Ian was running his rehearsals. Murder hadn't put a stop on the show. Ticket sales had gone up as predicted.

Londoners. We can be a macabre bunch when we want.

"Hello, darling. Finished poking around?"

"Yes. I've seen what I can for now, and I wouldn't want to get in anyone's way." Osian leaned in to whisper to Ian to avoid disturbing the rehearsal. "I'll be back tomorrow with Dannel, hopefully. Two heads are better than one."

"I've always thought so."

"*Ian.*" Osian ignored the salacious grin from the man and said his goodbyes.

Maybe I can surprise Dannel with an early tea.

Stopping by Meatliquor, Osian picked up onion rings, two cheeseburgers, and two of their biscoff shakes. Nothing said "I love you" like a greasy heart attack in a takeaway container. He was proud of himself for not grabbing deep-fried mac'n'cheese or more chicken wings than he could carry.

I am the epitome of restraint.

And a terrible liar.

"Hello, duckie."

Osian nodded to Adelle, who had her jaunty Thames on his leash. "Off for his afternoon walk, are you?"

"We are. Did Dannel's visit with his dad go well?" Adelle and Stanley had lived in the building for ages. They remembered back when Osian and Dannel were young lads living across the hall from one another. "We haven't seen Myron in ages. It's always a pleasant surprise."

Is it?

Poor Dannel, left alone to deal with Myron.

"I'm sure it went well." Osian wasn't completely confident of the opposite. He crouched down to pat Thames on the head, resisting his urge to rush upstairs. No need to be rude. "You two enjoy your walk. It's a lovely summer day."

"You take good care of your young man, duckie." Adelle patted him on the shoulder. "Go on, up to your Dannel."

Watching her meander down the pavement with Thames by her side, Osian couldn't help thinking he'd gotten so lucky. Both Dannel and he had been surrounded by supportive friends, family, and neighbours throughout their lives. Not idyllic; nothing in the real world could ever be perfectly pastoral perfection.

And certainly not in London.

It had, however, been almost magical.

Osian opened the front door, jogged up the stairs, and made his way into their flat. He slowed his step when he realised the curtains were pulled shut and all the lights had been turned out except for the glow of the telly. "Dannel?"

Silence.

Finding Dannel fast asleep on the couch, Osian left him to rest. Sometimes, nothing helped more than a nap. *And cake.* He spotted a Tupperware container on the coffee table.

At least we have the cake covered.

Of course, when do we ever not have cake handled.

Priorities.

Gathering up the mugs from the table, Osian set the food to one side and washed up the few dishes in the sink. He carried a stack of folded towels down the hall into the bedroom, checking on the drying shield. Dannel had finished up the paint and begun wrapping up the final embellishments.

Right.

Okay.

What do we need? Pyjamas, soft blankets, and comfort food.

"Ossie?"

Osian finished changing and grabbed Dannel's pyjamas and two blankets. He returned to the living room to find his boyfriend had followed his nose into the kitchen. "Good nap?"

Dannel shrugged.

Still waking up.

I can work with that.

"Here's your pj's." He held them out for Dannel. "We'll do a cosy video game day. Comfort food, lights down, blankets, and whatever game you want. The perfect way to wash the angst away."

Dannel eyed the pyjamas before grabbing them and changing in the kitchen, kicking his jeans and shirt to the side.

"I do like sausage and veg in the kitchen." He grinned when Dannel snorted. *Success. Stage one of lifting his spirits completed.* "Tea? Beer? Coke? Grab whatever drink you want. I'll plate up all this goodness I picked up for us. Don't forget the shakes in the fridge."

Experience told Osian not to press for conversation yet. Dannel would talk about his dad's visit when he was ready and not before. Pushing would only lead to his shutting down completely.

They sat on the floor around the coffee table, putting on a video game playthrough on YouTube to entertain them while eating. Dannel had grabbed a package of crisps, as onion rings weren't his favourite. They ate quietly.

"How did the theatre go?" Dannel finally emerged from his nap haze.

Osian shoved the onion ring in his hand into his mouth. "Oddly. I'll show you the ink stains I found on one of the costumes. Plus, the infamous ghost tried to lock me into Birdie's room."

"The ghost?" Dannel licked the ketchup dripping from his burger. "Can they turn locks?"

"This one did." Osian scoffed another onion ring. "The door slammed shut and wouldn't budge initially. By the time I got outside, no one was there."

"Suspicious, but not a proof of paranormal activity." He picked at the cheese on his burger.

"Why don't we stake out the theatre? Could Ian get us inside at night?"

"Probably. Or we could go high-tech with our paranormal investigation. I bet Chris could set us up with some of his spy gear." Osian figured a few hidden cameras might catch more than the ghost. "I'll text Abs to see if she knows where her boy toy is."

Chris Kirwin worked for a security company. He never talked about what he did. They knew he'd been in the military; Osian thought he got a thrill out of being mysterious.

The man had been instrumental in helping them solve Gemma's murder. He'd also saved Osian's life. It made him almost worthy of dating Abra, in Osian's opinion.

"Invite him to the dinner," Dannel suggested. He glanced into his cup and grumbled. "Why is it empty?"

"You drank it." Osian hid his grin by grabbing another onion ring. He casually slid his own shake across the table. "You can have the rest of mine."

"True. Love." Dannel mimicked one of their favourite movie moments.

"Okay, if you start talking like the priest from *Princess Bride*, I'm taking my shake back." Osian dug his phone out from under the stack of blankets. "Why don't we see if Roland and Wayne are still up for hosting the sing-a-long and interrogation of Archie tomorrow? Maybe they can sneak Chris onto the list if he isn't already."

"Abra's going to think you're meddling again."

"Who, me? Eh." Osian knew it would be entertaining to see Abra and Chris dance around each other. "What's the worst that can happen?"

"Famous last words." Dannel leaned against the edge of the sofa with a groan, shoving the coffee table away to get more space. "Biscoff shakes are deadly."

Slouching on the carpet together, they quietly watched the telly for a few minutes. Osian loved their quiet moments together. His favourite time of the day.

"You smell of onion." Dannel shoved Osian's head off his shoulder. "Disgusting."

Ahh, romance.

"Don't you want to cuddle with me?"

"Would you want to cuddle with a raw onion?" Dannel put a pillow in his face when Osian tried to lean toward him. "I love you unconditionally with fresh breath."

EIGHT

DANNEL

THE MAGICAL SCENT OF COFFEE DREW DANNEL OUT of bed. He rolled on his back, stretching out across the blankets. Osian had obviously gotten up early to walk with Abra and edit the podcast.

They were already a day behind on uploading the first part of the deep dive into the theatre mysteries. Dragging himself out of bed, Dannel trudged across the hall into their office. It did double duty as his creative space.

One of the first changes they'd made had been to exchange the desk for a proper cutting table. They'd found two drawer units at IKEA to use as the base and added a sturdy wooden top harvested from an old dining room table. It allowed them both to work in the space, cut all sorts of fabric, and offered a flat surface to photograph their creations.

Multiple shelves along the left wall were lined with containers filled with supplies. Finished creations went into the closet. Unique pieces, like a detailed weapon fabricated out of a Nerf gun, had been set on the walls as decoration.

The weapon had been part of Osian's Zaeed Massani cosplay from a few years back. Zaeed was from one of their favourite games from the Mass Effect trilogy. Dannel had been particularly proud of how Jessie, a replica of the character's weapon, had turned out.

On the wall closest to the door, they'd created a giant pinboard. Project ideas, character screenshots, and commission details were placed on it. They used it to keep on track of their growing business.

Or, as Olivia had claimed after helping them design the room, it added to the ambience.

Aesthetics.

She'd been the mastermind behind adding several extra lights, including one directly over the cutting table. Dannel appreciated them on grey days, of which London had many. She'd also brought in a Steampunk vibe with a few odds and ends around the room, items on the shelves, the slight golden tint to the paint on the walls, and a few extra pieces of artwork.

Dannel often felt like he went to work in a lab straight from a video game. "I can hear you breathing in the hallway."

"Your uncle Danny brought us a breakfast patty or five." Osian held up the cling film-covered plate. He stood by the door, watching him. "Breakfast?"

Patties were a classic Jamaican flaky pastry pie of sorts. His mum and his auntie Myriam made a breakfast version with spiced sausage, egg, and cheese. They often added diced potato.

"Your auntie Myriam made them. I've had four already."

"Greedy git."

Myriam and Dannel "Danny" Ortea owned both the building of flats as well as the shop on the ground floor. His uncle had looked after his sister, Rolina, and her two sons. Dannel looked up to the man more than he did his own father.

"Are we still going ghost hunting this morning?" Osian set the coffee down on the cutting table and leaned against it. "Chris is up for meeting us at the theatre. He's got the day off apparently. I invited Abs to come along as well."

Dannel snickered into his coffee. "I'll bring popcorn."

"She told me to sod off. Bit rude." Osian pulled the cling film off the plate and handed it to Dannel. "Eat up. We don't want to be too late."

Between finishing breakfast and showering together, which took longer than if they'd done so separately, they arrived quite late. Chris was standing outside the Evelyn Lavelle Theatre with an animated Ian chatting him up. Dannel elbowed Osian when he snickered.

"Fancy seeing you here, darlings." Ian waved coquettishly at them. He swatted Chris on the arm with his scarf. "This fine specimen has been keeping me company. Shall I let you into the theatre?"

"Probably a wise idea," Dannel muttered.

"Yes, please." Chris cursed under his breath, almost growling when Osian and Dannel snickered at the pleading in his voice. "Some days, I wonder why I saved your lives."

"No, you don't." Dannel glanced in Chris's direction. "Right. Joking. You were making a joke. I didn't laugh."

"Wasn't a funny joke." Osian threw his arm around Dannel's shoulders. "We've had lots of coffee this morning."

"And sex."

"They didn't need to know why we were late." Osian choked out a laugh.

"Git." Dannel pinched the bridge of his nose, trying to stave off the flush of embarrassment. "The Matrix is glitching this morning."

"You can't blame the Matrix for your verbal explosions." Osian grabbed his side, laughing so hard he almost tipped over. "Verbal explosions."

"If you two nerds are quite finished?" Chris nodded to where Ian had already headed inside the theatre. "Though I'm happy to see Ian's distracted."

"You're a fine specimen," Osian teased.

"I can leave, you know." Chris reached down to grab the duffle at his feet. "I brought several of these small cameras, including one with thermal imaging. They're motion-activated as well. I've wanted a chance to test them out."

Osian hummed the *Ghostbusters* theme while they made their way down to Birdie's room. Caution tape lay on the floor. "Ian?"

"Yes, darling?"

Osian knelt down to pick up the bright yellow tape. "Have the police finished up?"

"I haven't the foggiest." Ian opened the door and stretched his arm out to flick the lights on.

"Well, goodness me. It didn't look like this yesterday."

Ruined costumes littered the room. Chris stepped up, blocking all three of them from stepping inside the room. They could clearly see the damage, even without going inside.

Dannel let out a low whistle while they crowded the doorframe to view the frenzied destruction of all the intricate costumes Birdie and her assistants had created. "Is the ghost a deceased Edward Scissorhands?"

"Chris," Osian whined playfully. "Let us at least take some photos before Haider runs us off."

Chris narrowed his eyes before nodding. "Don't touch *anything*. I'm not explaining why your grubby prints are everywhere."

"My fingers are clean." Dannel scrutinized his hands. "Haider already cleared us. If anything, he'll be hacked off we poked our nose into the investigation."

While Chris called the police, Osian and Dannel tried to inspect the room around the tall, human impediment in their way. It appeared someone had gone out of their way to destroy every costume for the play. Ian stood with a hand on his chest; and his other covered his mouth in shock.

"Ian?" Osian caught him by the arm, holding him up when he seemed to go faint. "Are you all right? Why don't we find somewhere for you to sit down? Come on. I'll help you to your dressing room."

"Ghost," Ian whispered.

"Whatever or whoever it is, I promise we'll stop them." Osian glanced back at Dannel before leading the weak Ian down the hall.

Chris pocketed his phone and leaned against the doorway. "Detective Inspectors Khan and Powell are on their way. They hadn't released the scene yet, so no one should've been inside."

Dannel shifted awkwardly in the hallway. He reached into his backpack to pull out his camera; they'd upgraded it to get better shots for their website. "Think the police would mind if I took a few photos?"

"Probably." Chris stepped out of the way. "Go on. I imagine the façade of a dinner party tonight will love to get a closer look at the crime scene."

Dannel took a quick video of the crime scene first and then began to get zoomed-in shots of every angle possible. "Façade. We're going to have actual food. It's a singalong with food and a side of Cluedo. *Git.*"

"Nerd."

"Hardly an insult." Dannel probably had worn his nerd badge long before the world decided they were cool. "Chris?"

"Yes, nerd?" Chris grinned at him. His smile fell away at the look at Dannel's face. "What? I was only joking."

"No, don't be daft as well as a git." Dannel pointed into the room. A glint off one of the dress forms had caught his eye through the lens. "Someone's stabbed scissors into the back. A message from the killer?"

"To whom?"

He had a point. Birdie was already dead. Using a similar weapon plunged into a dress form sent a warning, but the question was: who had been the intended recipient?

Ian? Us? The police? Doubtful. Someone else in the company?

"It's not over, is it?" Dannel put the cap on his camera and carefully stored it in his bag. "Bugger. Am I reading too much into a pair of scissors?"

"Not when they're stabbing the back of a red garment draped on a mannequin." Chris caught him by the shoulder to ease him away from the door. "I imagine the police will be here shortly. Let's not make it obvious we snooped."

NINE

OSIAN

After settling Ian in his dressing room with hot tea and a cadre of his theatre admirers to soothe his nerves, Osian decided to sneak around backstage before the police arrived. He saw no evidence of an intruder. The sound of running footsteps drew him deeper into the building toward a set of stairs leading into the basement.

Nothing. Someone genuinely wants everyone to believe there's a ghost. Bellend. What are they getting from this?

They can't honestly believe the police will stop investigating a murder and try for an exorcism instead.

What absolute rubbish.

Osian went halfway down the stairs towards the darkened basement where old props were stored.

"You know, maybe I'll wait for Haider. They're getting paid to investigate."

I don't believe in ghosts, but a little caution never hurt anyone.

Taking the steps two at a time, Osian jogged back to Dannel and Chris. He found them mid-conversation with the two detective inspectors, who didn't seem thrilled by the invasion of their crime scene. *What a surprise.*

Or maybe it was Dannel's unwillingness to chat with them.

Time for an intervention.

"Hello, Detectives." Osian sidled up to Dannel, casually drawing attention away from him. He could tell Dannel was teetering on the edge of being overstimulated. "Fancy meeting you here. Have you seen the destruction of your crime scene? Not very secure, now was it?"

"Mr Garey." Detective Inspector Powell had definitely reached the limit of her patience for the day. "We'd intended to release the crime scene this morning as it was."

The "not that it's any of your business" was left unsaid. Osian smiled brightly. He'd always found it the perfect way to distract from any situation.

Smile.

People never know how to react.

"Music." Dannel fished into his backpack and pulled out his earbuds. He wandered off down the hall with them firmly in his ears. "Bye."

Osian shifted into the centre of the hallway. If Dannel wanted space, he'd get it. *The detectives can bugger off if they've a problem with it.* "So, what do you make of the slice and dice job done to Birdie's costumes? Odd, isn't it?"

"We can't comment on an ongoing investigation." Detective Inspector Khan tried to maintain a stern glare in the face of Osian's forceful grin. "Did you touch anything?"

"Aside from myself or Dannel?" Osian ignored Chris, who coughed violently and turned away from them. He peered into the room. "Nope. We arrived this morning and stayed outside like the good lads we are. You might find the stabby scissors of particular interest."

"Osian." Haider lost his battle and chuckled. "Stabby scissors?"

"You can't miss them." He pointed toward the dress form. "Sinister placement."

"*Osian.*"

With one last grin for the detectives, Osian dragged Chris down the hallway toward the back stairs. He wanted reinforcements while he tried to hunt down the ghost. *Not that I believe in paranormal hauntings.*

"Where are we going?" Chris followed him, hesitating at the top of the steps. "Any particular reason we're going into a dark basement?"

"Ossie's afraid of ghosts." Dannel sat further down the hall. He had his earbuds in his hand. "I'm guessing he heard something again."

"Well, we obviously can't string up cameras with the detectives all over the dressing rooms. Let's see what we've got in the basement in the meantime." Chris shifted his bag from one arm to the other. "I'm getting tired of lugging all this equipment around."

"With those muscles?" Osian chose to ignore Dannel's comment about the ghosts. He decided to needle Chris instead. "Come on, granddad. Let's get downstairs so we can get around to putting up the cameras."

"What are you expecting to find down here other than dusty curtains and props?" Chris followed Osian, who pulled Dannel along for the ride. They went down the two flights of stairs, through the squeaky doors into the storage area. "Think they used this as an air raid shelter? It's sturdy."

"No clue. The building's old enough." Osian fumbled around before finding the light switch. He blinked to get accustomed to the sudden brightness. A grey object partially hidden underneath an old set of stage curtains caught his eye. "What are you? Why in the world is there a Bluetooth speaker down here? No one's listening to music in this dusty tomb."

"One of the cast trying to rehearse in peace and quiet?" Dannel suggested. "It's where I'd go. I doubt anyone comes down here very often from the thick layer of dust."

Osian crouched down to inspect underneath the curtain further. "Nothing else here aside from the speaker."

"Not sure I call this nothing." Dannel gestured toward all of the stacks of old posters, curtains, props, and even a few costumes on clothing racks. "I wouldn't say this is empty."

"Nothing connected to this." Osian flung it halfway across the room a second later when the lights flickered and an ear-piercing shriek came out of the speaker. "What the actual—"

"So, I'm definitely adding one of my cameras to the staircase pointing at this room." Chris went over to retrieve the speaker. "I might ask Detective Inspector Khan to see what he makes of this."

"Right. And we should do that. Upstairs." Osian had already started for the door with Dannel close behind. "Don't pretend you're not at least a little bit uneasy about ghosts."

"If ghosts existed, there would be irrefutable proof by now," Dannel argued.

"They're elusive."

"If you're done with your commentary on whether shadow figures exist in real life?" Chris encouraged them to move forward.

They walked quickly. Osian was amused by how rapidly they all made their way up the stairs without actually breaking into a run. A calm stampede, of sorts, to get away from the ghost none of them wanted to admit to believing in.

"We'll mention the speaker. Not the ghost. Or our flight away from it." Osian didn't think either detective would buy into the paranormal. He still didn't. There had to be a logical explanation for what they were seeing at the Evelyn Lavelle Theatre. "Agreed?"

"Fair enough." Chris shrugged while Dannel nodded.

The two detectives had already wrapped up their inspection of the room. Haider held a bag with the scissors. They'd closed the door, adding caution tape for a second time.

Bugger.

We'll have to wait for them to leave before we can sneak Chris's cameras inside.

They'll ask too many questions otherwise.

Maybe we should wait to mention the speaker.

"We're off. Try to stay out of trouble." Haider seemed to focus his pointedly at Osian. "I'm serious. Let's not be in a rush to throw ourselves into danger."

"And by 'ourselves,' he means you three." Detective Inspector Powell tended to be more direct than her partner. "All right? I'm not eager to run down alibis for you again. We've more pressing things to focus our attention on."

"Us three? You mean those two," Chris protested. "You should know we—"

"No honour among thieves, eh?" Osian nudged

the taller man in the back to shut him up. "Wanker."

"We'll stay out of trouble." Dannel, ever the voice of reason, dragged Osian down the hall, waving a muttered goodbye at the two detectives. "They'll never leave if you keep playing the Joker."

"Which Joker? *Batman, Mass Effect, Batman* again?" Osian stumbled along behind his boyfriend, snickering the entire way. They'd left Chris to speak with Haider. "I vote for *Mass Effect.*"

"You just want to play Commander Shepard again." Dannel came to a stop once they'd gone around the corner. "We'll hide until the police have gone."

"I'm Commander Shepard, and this is my favourite hall in the theatre to snog in." Osian leaned in for a kiss. "I've had a brush with death. I feel alive."

"A ghostly erection?" Dannel said with a perfectly straight face.

A sharp laugh from the right told them Chris had finished his goodbyes with the detectives. He was leaning against the wall, trying to catch his breath. Osian extracted himself from Dannel.

"Ghostly erection. A whole new meaning to probing the paranormal." Osian decided to change the subject, or they'd never get anything accomplished. "Detectives gone, then?"

"I told them about the speaker despite your trying to stop me. They're going to check it out later. I got the distinct feeling they thought it was merely a prank." Chris slowly regained his composure and stopped laughing between sentences. "Haider left strict instructions to *not* enter the costume design studio or poke your noses into the investigation at all."

"So? Where are we putting cameras first?" Osian had no intentions of obstructing the police. They were there to figure out the paranormal aspect. A story he fully planned on sticking to if asked. "The stairwell?"

"Why don't I head out to the lobby? I can make sure the police don't unexpectedly return and figure out what we're doing." Dannel plugged his earbuds in. "Might want to be quick in case whoever's faking the ghost spots what you're doing."

If the ghost is a fake.

It's probably a fake.

Osian watched him disappear through the doors down the hall. He glanced over at Chris, who'd pulled several tiny cameras out of his bag. "Bond, James Bond."

"More like Q than Bond." Chris handed four of them to Osian. "Hang on to these for me so I have a hand free."

Juggling the multiple cameras and Chris's bag, Osian retraced their steps to the stairwell. He kept a watch for any signs of anyone with the theatre company. *Or a ghost.* Chris did a thorough check of the area before finding an out of the way spot to secure the first spycam.

Osian waited for Chris to finish before offering him the second camera. He twisted the spherical gadget around; it fit easily in the palm of his hand. "Tiny things, aren't they?"

"Nanny cams, really. A lot of parents use them to keep an eye on their kids. Hard to spot if you know what you're doing." Chris guided him to the end of the hallway. "This one'll give us a view of anyone going near the room or the stairs. Never know what we'll see."

People snogging, if Dannel and I are an example.

What happens in the theatre stays in the theatre.

"What are the odds whoever's haunting us has a camera as well? It would explain how they knew when someone is nearby." Osian preferred not to consider the ghost might be real. "Or should I work on finding an exorcist?"

"I've looked carefully for any signs of a camera but not seen anything. There's CCTV at the front of the theatre. It's possible someone's hacked into those to keep an eye on anyone inside. Also, the building's an old, creaky thing. Who's to say they're not hearing when someone's on the stairs or going through a specific part of the hallway?" Chris finished hiding the second one in the corner and held his hand out for a third. "We'll put the last two into the room itself, since someone's obviously still interested."

And we'll never ever mention it to Haider.

He'll be so disappointed—unless we find evidence of the killer and then he'll only pretend to be annoyed.

It didn't take long at all to hide the remaining cameras. Chris promised to help him set up the feed on his laptop at dinner that evening. He'd already agreed to the invitation.

Abs will be thrilled.

Or kill me.

"Try not to get yourselves locked in any rooms this time, all right?" Chris said his goodbyes, heading out of the theatre. "See you this evening."

"Ready?" Dannel sat on the floor across from the ticket booths.

Osian slid to the floor to sit beside him. "Why

don't we see how rehearsals are going before we leave? Poor Ian. I wonder what they'll do, with his costume designer murdered and all the costumes destroyed."

"Postpone?"

"Can you see Ian postponing his precious play?" Osian had a feeling Ian would rather bankrupt himself hiring an army of costumers to recreate all of Birdie's designs in time. They paused outside the doors, listening to the rehearsal. Ian sounded far more frenzied than they'd ever heard him. "Why don't we check on him later?"

"Probably wise." Dannel was already moving away from the door. "We'll only disrupt the process."

"Why don't we check on Archie instead? See if he's up for dinner tonight." Osian hadn't heard from their friend even after sending him several texts. "He's staying at his mum's place. It's just a few streets away. We can grab a coffee when we're done."

Despite the summer heat, Osian enjoyed their walk. He'd always loved the hustle and bustle of the West End. They dodged around a small group of fans belting out one of their favourite songs while watching for the cast to arrive.

Just another day in Covent Garden.

"Ossie." Dannel caught him by the elbow to stop him walking across the street. "Look."

"What?" Osian finally spotted Archie and his boyfriend having a fantastic row on the steps up to the flat. "Trouble in paradise. Maybe we should say hello."

"In the middle of an argument?"

"How else are we going to eavesdrop?" Osian caught him by the hand before jogging across the street and dodging traffic. "It's a friendly coincidence."

They reached the shouting couple just in time for the end of the argument. Niall stormed off with a curse and a rude gesture. Archie stared gloomily after him.

"Arch? Everything all right?" Osian darted forward when Archie's legs seemed to go out from under him. "Why don't we get you inside, yeah? A cup of tea, a biscuit, and a chat with friends. Or we can chase down the git and knock some sense into him."

"Nah. Leave him alone." Archie shook his head. He managed to stand up straight, pushing Osian gently away. "Come up, then. You nosy prat. I need some green tea."

The flat was all Birdie. Stacks of fabrics, ribbon, and sketch pads covered most flat surfaces. Storage containers lined the hallway and one of the living room walls. A sewing machine took up the entire space by the front window, offering a lovely view from where she must've worked.

There were stray buttons across the coffee table, as if Birdie had been searching for a specific one. Archie had obviously not changed much of anything since his mum's death. Osian exchanged a glance with Dannel.

"Have you thought about getting someone in to help you with your mum's stuff?" Dannel asked hesitantly. "Just to box it up?"

Danny.

Trying not to drop his face into his hands, Osian tried to figure out how to delicately ease their way through the conversation minefield. It had only been a few days since her death. Archie probably wasn't ready to even consider boxing his mum's stuff away.

Osian decided to pretend to ignore the matter completely when Archie began to look a little teary-eyed. *Time for a delicately phrased change of subject.* "Why don't we have some of your green tea?"

I am a master of subtlety.

"Niall and I broke up."

"Ah." Dannel seemed to be floundering for something to say. "Why?"

Well, it's not how I would've asked, but I am curious.

Archie sank tiredly onto the teal velvet settee that definitely evoked his mum's Victorian aesthetic. "I think he killed my mum."

TEN
DANNEL

IN THE SILENCE FOLLOWING HIS STATEMENT, ARCHIE had disappeared into the kitchen. He returned ten minutes later with a tray of delicate rose teacups and a matching platter with slices of a sticky ginger loaf cake. It had given Dannel and Osian time to consider how to broach the subject of his accusing Niall of murder.

"Arch." Osian had already scoffed down half a slice of cake. He took a sip of tea and immediately spat it back into the cup.

"Ossie." Dannel grimaced. "You weren't actually raised by wolves, no matter what your mum says."

"What is this?" Osian stared down into his tea,

then set the cup carefully down on the tray. "Pond water?"

"A loose blend I purchased in a village outside of Kathmandu." Archie sipped his slowly. "An acquired taste."

"Acquired by hobbits, maybe." Osian grabbed another slice of cake. "Really, Arch? You couldn't have stretched to maybe a simple breakfast tea or something?"

"Do hobbits drink mulchy tea?" Dannel grimaced through a sip.

Before they could continue their conversation about Niall, the doorbell rang, followed by an impatient knock. Dannel wondered if the man in question had returned to continue the argument. Archie clearly had the same thought when he rushed to answer the door.

"Mr Dennis. Mind if we come in for a chat?" Detective Inspector Khan's distinctive voice drifted through the flat.

Dannel and Osian both shot to their feet as they heard Archie inviting the police inside. "He's going to think we're interfering."

"We are." Osian snagged a third slice of cake. "One for the road. You know they'll kick us out."

"Ah." Haider paused for half a second before

continuing into the living room. "Why am I not surprised to see you two?"

"Just offering our support to a good friend during this sad time." Osian sounded far more believable than Dannel thought possible. "We were having a spot of tea."

"Perhaps you might see yourself out while we have a private conversation with Mr Dennis?" Haider stared pointedly at the two of them.

"I'd rather they stay." Archie scooted around the two detectives into the room. "Care for tea? I can reheat the kettle. And there's plenty of cake."

"No, thank you." Haider didn't take a seat. "We'd actually like you to come with us for a more official conversation. We've had contact with someone who claims you admitted to killing your mother."

"Well, Niall works fast." Osian pulled his phone out of his pocket. "Wayne might like to meet you at the police station, Archie. I wouldn't speak with the detective inspectors until he's arrived."

"Niall?" Archie glanced over at Osian in a bit of a haze. He didn't seem to be processing what was happening. "I don't understand."

"You accused your boyfriend of killing your mother. He's obviously gone and told our dear friends here that you've done it as a pre-emptive strike." Dannel caught on quickly to what Osian had seen. It certainly wasn't a stretch. "Clever bastard."

"We obviously can't disclose any witness statements. We'd simply like you to come with us for a friendly chat." Inspector Powell entered the conversation with a forced smile. "If you would?"

"If it's a friendly chat, why doesn't he meet you there in an hour?" Osian pocketed his phone, having finished his text conversation. "It's always lovely to see you, Detectives. How about I see you out for Archie, who's obviously still distraught over the loss of his mum?"

The two detective inspectors seemed to have a silent conversation with each other. Haider reluctantly nodded, insisting on Archie presenting himself to them for questioning within the hour. They left the flat with an air of frustration.

"Thank you." Archie smothered Osian and Dannel in a hug, his long arms squashing them to him. "Thank you. Thank. You."

"Thank me with a cup of tea. A nice strong one. Or coffee." Osian struggled out from the hug.

Dannel followed his example, feeling as though

a desperate octopus had clung to them. "Is Wayne coming here?"

"He said to give him twenty minutes. He's finishing up with another client." Osian flopped into one of the fancy armchairs. "Archie. You're going to need to be honest with Wayne."

"About?" Archie scowled at Osian while gathering up the cups and plate. "I didn't hurt my mum."

Stomping out of the room into the kitchen, Archie left them to their own devices. Osian held his finger up to his mouth and tiptoed over to Birdie's sewing table. He flicked through a stack of papers on one corner.

"Ossie," Dannel whispered. He kept an eye on the door into the kitchen for any sign of movement. "*Ossie.*"

"Shh." Osian used his phone to snap a photo of one of the pieces of paper. He quickly returned the documents to their original state and rushed back over to Dannel. "Remember the hat lady?"

"From the funeral?"

Osian showed the photo on his phone. "She sent the quintessential strongly worded letter about being fired."

"Does it involve threats of stabbing with scissors?" Dannel tried to read the tiny script. He almost dropped the phone when Archie returned from the kitchen. "Why did you think Niall murdered your mum?"

Osian nudged him in the side.

"What?" Dannel was genuinely confused. They'd asked earlier, but the police had interrupted the conversation. "We might as well kill time waiting for Wayne to arrive."

"Kill time?"

"Don't pick apart my words." Dannel frowned at Osian, who offered a muttered apology. He glanced over at Archie. "We don't have to talk about your mum. Or your boyfriend."

Though it would answer loads of our questions.

Archie sat so absently on the sofa, Dannel worried he'd hit the floor instead. "I've no proof. You know me, I've never really seen the worst in anyone even when they deserved it. He did argue something awful with Mum. Her accusation hurt his feelings. I don't know if I'd called it a gut instinct, but who else could've done it?"

"Is it possible Niall did cheat on you?" Dannel hadn't spent any time at all with Archie's boyfriend (or ex-boyfriend); he still managed to give him a bad vibe. "Your mum never struck me as the sort to make up an accusation for fun."

"She wasn't. And he didn't," Archie stated emphatically. "You haven't had a chance to get to know him."

And I'm not sure I want to. That's not nice. I should give him a chance. He just seems so smarmy.

So smarmy.

So smarmy I feel like I need a shower after a single conversation about him.

Is it wrong to judge him without having spent time with him? Probably. There's just something about him.

The conversation fell away. Archie wasn't willing to answer any more questions. Dannel wondered how things would go if he clammed up in front of the police as well.

When Wayne arrived, he headed out with Archie, insisting on requiring privacy with his client. Dannel and Osian found themselves on the pavement watching the two drive off together. *Well, now what?*

"Home?" Osian wrapped his arm around Dannel's shoulders. "We have a podcast to research. I want to do another episode on the criminal side of the theatre in London."

"To distract yourself from whatever's happening with Archie?"

"Of course." Osian coughed several times. "Maybe pick up some coffee on the way home. I swear I've got twigs stuck in my throat."

"Tea leaves. Not twigs."

"Semantics."

"Tea leaves. Not. Twigs," Dannel insisted. He couldn't help being pedantic with words. They mattered. They had meaning. "Maybe a stray flower."

"We could—"

"No." Dannel knew that particular tone of Osian's. He might not always understand the nuance of conversation, but he knew his boyfriend. "We're not going to the police station."

"We'd be supporting a friend."

"We'd be shoving our noses too far into the investigation. So far we might get them cut off. Don't be a daft twit." Dannel jostled Osian to the side to avoid barging into a woman struggling down the sidewalk with her three children. "We'll see Archie and Wayne at the dinner party tonight. I'm sure they'll tell us all about the visit to the police station without having to risk Haider's ire."

"Fine." Osian paused on the corner, waiting for

several cars to go by and then jogging across the street with Dannel. "Remember the old doorman at the theatre?"

"Chester?"

"Lester?"

Dannel stopped walking and tried to think back to the cheerful old bloke who bore a striking resemblance to Santa, complete with a long beard and round tummy. "Bob."

"You sure an 'ester' wasn't involved somewhere?"

Dannel snickered with Osian. "Maybe not Bob. Something benignly normal."

"Brigham Green." Osian stopped in the middle of the pavement. "That was his name. I remember now. We always teased him about being a puritan."

"Yes, Brigham. Completely normal-sounding name." Dannel tried to remember when they'd seen him last. "Where'd he go after retiring?"

"No idea. I do know he liked walking his dog in the same park as Adelle and Stanley. Why don't we have a peek on the way home? Maybe he's there." Osian intertwined his fingers with Dannel's while they continued walking. "I'm thinking he might have some theatre gossip for us. He's still coming by the Evelyn Lavelle to help Ian from time to time and knows absolutely everyone."

Dannel paused for a second, trying to recall something Evie had told him once. "Didn't Brigham and Birdie have an affair once? Like ten years ago or something?"

"Maybe he's Archie's real dad."

"Brigham isn't ginger."

"Well, he's grey-haired now. He might've been ginger in a previous life." Osian occasionally had a far too vivid imagination. "Seriously, though, maybe it's not Archie's relationship causing the problems. Maybe it was Birdie's. We could ask. You should ask him."

"Don't throw me in front of the firing line for awful questions. I am *not* going to ask Archie about his mum's sex life." Dannel shuddered. *Is there a more awkward topic of conversation? Probably.* "Why don't we see if we can find Brigham? Maybe we can find a subtle way to fit Birdie into the conversation."

"Us? Subtle? Sure."

ELEVEN

OSIAN

At school, Osian had found nothing more boring than doing research for a paper. He'd done better with practical over theory. As an adult, he thrived in falling down Wikipedia rabbit holes while exploring a subject for their podcast.

"Want to go to the Adelphi?" Osian stretched his leg out to kick Dannel lightly in the side. "Quit ignoring me."

"I'm trying to solve this puzzle." Dannel had been playing a new game for hours. He was starting to tense up out of frustration. "I'm so close."

"You're close to rage quitting. Hit the save button. We've got a little over an hour before we need to leave for the dinner party. Do you really want to get all wound up right now?" Osian waited patiently for Dannel to mull his advice over. "Tomorrow, though. Want to go with me to the Adelphi theatre? I want to see if we can spot William Terriss's ghost. And get a few photographs for the podcast thumbnail."

"William Terriss?"

"Think the 1800s version of Errol Flynn. He was murdered at the stage door by a fellow actor in 1897, who barely got a slap on the wrist. Terriss's ghost supposedly haunts the Adelphi and the Covent Garden tube station." Osian typed out a few notes in a Word document. He thought a deep dive into the case might prove fascinating enough for an entire podcast episode of its own. "There's a twisted history between the two."

"Isn't there always?" Dannel saved his game and tossed his controller onto the sofa with a disgruntled groan. "Did Stanley text you about Brigham?"

"They haven't seen him in a few days." Osian finished up his thoughts for their next podcast, hit save, and closed his laptop. "What are we going to do about Ian's ghost?"

"Compel him to stop?"

"I only cosplay as John Constantine." Osian stretched out on the sofa, trying to work the kinks out of his back. "I'm not sure I can fight off a real paranormal being."

"Did you say real and paranormal in the same sentence with a straight face?"

"You know what I meant."

"Nope." Dannel dodged the pillow Osian chucked at him. "We've got the cameras set up now. Chris gave us access to the live feed. All we can do is watch and see."

Dressing for a dinner party mostly involved flinging socks at each other until the room looked like a fabric octopus had been segmented in a strange horror film. Evie interrupted their battle. They had to rush to finish changing in time for their Uber.

They had the driver swing by Abra's building to pick her up. She brought a fresh batch of strawberry jelly shots, a heady combination of berry gelatin with lime margarita mix and tequila. Osian had a feeling they'd arrive at Wayne's swanky flat already quite sloshed.

The football chants started five minutes away from the flat. Chelsea versus Tottenham, of course. Abra and Osian enjoyed needling Dannel and Evie about their club. He had no doubt the poor Uber driver was happy to be shot of them by the time they'd starting singing Frank Lampard's praises.

"Think we made a friend." Osian watched the car drive off as quickly as possible. "He won't be taking a ride from our place ever again."

They sang their way up the elevator and down the hall. Osian wondered how many complaints Wayne was going to get from his neighbours. *We don't even have a decent excuse for our raucous behaviour.*

"Are you lot quite finished trying to get me evicted for noise complaints?" Wayne bundled them into the flat. "We've got a boatload of pizza. Eat something. How do you get sozzled on the drive here?"

"Tequila on an empty stomach. And we're not 'sozzled,' you posh prat." Abra squeezed by them into the flat and immediately went straight for the spread of food on the table. "I'd say we're giggly if anything."

"Rolly." Osian waved at Dannel's younger brother, who appeared to be setting out plates. *How adorable.* "How goes the detecting?"

"It's Roland." He was so easy to rile up. "And I'm not a detective yet."

"Do you have monogrammed towels yet?" Osian asked when Roland fished around in a nearby cabinet for glasses. "Should we have the talk with Wayne, so he doesn't break your poor heart?"

"Osian." Roland pointed a folded napkin at him, which only served to make him laugh uproariously. "Must you do this? Neither you nor Dannel have bothered any of my previous dates, whether man or woman."

"Yes, but Wayne's your one true love. The unrequited love you dreamed about at uni," Osian teased.

"I hate you." Roland pointed a fork at him. "Oi. Dannel. Retrieve your person so I don't have to chuck him out a window."

"Fairly certain the police frown on chucking people out windows."

"They'd make an exception for you." He returned to spreading out the pizza boxes. "Think we've got enough?"

"To feed an entire army?" Osian counted at least twelve boxes. "We can always order more. Is everyone coming?"

A knock on the door interrupted their conversation. Archie arrived, followed surprisingly by his boyfriend, Niall. *Well, well, well, what an interesting development. Have they forgiven mutual accusations of murder? Or was that a diversion?*

The more true crime Osian researched, the more suspicious of people he became. Archie had never shown himself to be devious. But he'd also been off travelling to discover himself.

Maybe he'd discovered an inner murderer.

Dannel snuck away from the various introductions and sidled up to Osian, who was watching Archie and Niall across the room. "Weird, right?"

"Distinctly," Osian agreed readily. "Who apologised to whom?"

"No idea. They could've arrived separately but come up in the elevator together."

"I doubt it. No way Rolly or Wayne invited him on his own. They came together. It's weird." Osian thought both men appeared tense. "We'll see if we can get the others to separate them without being obvious. You can ask Archie what's going on while I prod Niall to see if he loses his temper again."

Though, given their standoffish body language, Osian wondered if they'd even need to prod Niall. The couple might've arrived together, but they seemed to have a permanent wedge keeping them at least slightly apart from one another. No touching, not even by accident. As if they were maintaining the façade of a relationship, yet fractured sufficiently to make it impossible to show genuine warmth.

And the mood between the two seemed almost frigid.

"Dannel?" Roland waved his brother over to where he'd been trying to decide what music they were going to pick.

With the brothers busy, Wayne disengaged from his conversation and joined Osian at the table. He nodded his head toward the kitchen. They stepped inside, and Wayne shut the door behind him.

"I'm not interested in boyfriend swapping." Osian held a hand up in front of him. "You're not my type."

"Male?"

"Posh prat with a swanky flat." Osian grinned.

"And whiny paramedic with a podcast isn't my type. Now we've got that out of the way." Wayne rolled his eyes. He went over to the fridge to retrieve two bottles of wine. "Listen, attorney-client privilege means I can't discuss details of what happened at the police station."

Odd.

I haven't even asked yet.

Osian tried to decipher what Wayne was trying

to dance around. "Right. I'm aware. You were my solicitor."

"Niall *isn't* my client." Wayne put an emphasis on specific words. "He showed up at the interview much to my surprise to offer his *support*. Archie apparently texted him out of stress."

"Did he now?" Osian didn't think he'd be willing to stand by someone who'd recently accused him of murder. "Suspicious, considering the amazing row I witnessed between him and Arch. Well, to be fair, maybe not suspicious, but it's odd."

"Be careful, all right?" Wayne rested a hand on Osian's shoulder, squeezing gently. "I'd tell you to not get involved but when have you ever listened to my advice?"

"I listen." Osian had certainly taken Wayne's advice during his brush with the police. "I do. Quit laughing at me."

For an evening fraught with the potential for drama, Osian found himself highly disappointed. Niall and Archie portrayed a loving couple in the midst of a mild disagreement perfectly. Neither of them opened up even the slightest despite his best attempts.

Chris hadn't shown. A work emergency of some sort. Abra shoved a handful of ice down Osian's back to stop his teasing about being stood up. *I might've deserved that one.*

The party broke up after midnight. Abra and Evie headed off together, intending to join mutual friends at a dance club. Archie and Niall slunk off soon after, ignoring Osian's offer to share an Uber.

"Here. We'll help clean up." Dannel shoved Osian toward the mess in the living room. "Grab the glasses. I'll take the plates."

"So, what have we learned?" Roland joined them in the kitchen, helping wash while Dannel dried. "Wayne can't share his thoughts, but if I were one of the detective inspectors on the case. I'd certainly be keeping an eye on both Niall and Archie."

"Even Archie?" Osian didn't want to believe the worst of a friend and fellow paramedic, someone who'd dedicated much of his time to helping others. "The gentle ginger giant? Who's discovered his inner peace and twig tea?"

"Ossie." Dannel motioned for him to set the plates in the sink. "Maybe Niall did it and Archie's covering for him? He might not want to lose his mum and his boyfriend at the same time."

"How long has this bloke even been in his life?"

Roland sounded as suspicious as Osian felt about Niall. "Months?"

"Love at first sight?" Wayne eased into the kitchen with his arms filled with empty boxes of pizza. "I officially have no comment on the subject."

"Maybe." Osian doubted love had anything to do with it. "Birdie thought Niall cheated on him."

"Birdie wouldn't have taken anyone hurting her son lightly." Dannel handed another dish to his brother to dry. "We should've asked more questions."

"Oh. Now you want to ask questions. You told me not to be pushy." Osian helped Wayne stack the dry dishes.

"You were rude." Dannel shrugged.

"Yeah, Oz. Rude." Roland smirked over his shoulder at Osian.

"Shut it, Roly Poly." Osian headed out into the living room to pick up a few stray utensils they'd missed. He returned to find Dannel on his own. "Abandoned in your time of need?"

"They're snogging." Dannel wrinkled his nose. "Not something I want to see my baby brother doing."

"He's twenty-seven and a copper."

"Do you want to watch your baby sister snog her husband?"

"Fair point." Osian didn't want to think about Olivia snogging. She might be a tiara-wearing Boadicea, ready to conquer the world, but some things a brother didn't need to see. "Did you hear Niall mention his plans for tomorrow?"

"Flat hunting."

"Wonder if we can accidentally run into him. Ask a few pointed questions." Osian decided to text Archie in the morning to see if he'd spill the beans on his current or ex-boyfriend, whatever the case happened to be. "Ready to go home?"

Dannel tossed the tea towel onto the counter. "Sure. They'll be ages."

They made their way out of the flat, making sure to yell out their goodbyes. Osian dragged Dannel into a snog of their own once inside the elevator. He didn't mind giving the CCTV operator a tiny thrill.

Dannel stepped out of the elevator and froze. He dragged Osian around the corner. "Niall and Archie. They're still outside."

"What?" Osian peeked around the corner. "We were upstairs for ages after they left. How have they not gone home?"

"Ossie."

"You wanted me to be less subtle." Osian ignored him, stepping out and striding out of the building. He put on a bright, cheerful face when Archie and Niall stopped talking. "Hello. Fancy meeting you here."

"I was just leaving." Niall jogged off down the street, leaving Archie to stare uncomfortably after him.

"Something I said?"

Archie shook his head and sighed heavily. He shoved his hands into his pockets, kicking at a stray pebble on the ground. "Hard to repair your relationship when you accuse each other of murder."

"True." Osian wondered if Archie was having second thoughts. "Do you think he's innocent?"

"Dunno."

"Does he think you're innocent?"

"Dunno."

Osian rubbed his forehead. He'd had a little too much wine and not enough sleep to deal with relationship troubles when a murder was in the mix. "Maybe you should figure out if he's guilty before you shag him senseless in your mum's flat."

"*Ossie.*"

TWELVE
DANNEL

THE FOLLOWING MORNING A HUNGOVER OSIAN dragged himself out of bed to meet up with his mum and stepdad for breakfast. Dannel slept in until insistent knocking woke him up. He trudged to the front door, fully prepared to have a go at whoever had interrupted his lie in.

"What the devil did you tell Archie last night after I left?"

Dannel blinked blearily at Niall. *How's he know where we live?* "I'm in pyjamas. Why are you shouting?"

Niall was silent for a full minute. "Sorry."

"Coffee." Dannel didn't want Niall in their personal space. "Wait here."

Shutting the door in the bewildered Niall's face,

Dannel retracted his steps to the bedroom. He changed quickly out of his pyjamas into his workout gear since it was handy. *I can do this. Ossie practised questions with me. Inside voice, just remember to use your inside voice.*

Count the eye contact. Several seconds, then look away. Don't make it odd.

Inside voice.

No matter how hard Dannel tried, he always struggled at knowing how loud his voice was. It had led to many embarrassing moments over the years. Talking too quietly or practically shouting without being aware. It frustrated him.

He adjusted his T-shirt and sweatpants, shoving his feet into his trainers. They'd get a coffee. He'd ask questions and then go for a run to release the tension, hopefully avoiding another meltdown.

Not the way Dannel had intended to spend his morning. He had several emails he needed to respond to along with a query on a commission. One of their friends wanted a set of armour similar to one from the video game *Thief*.

Dannel had never played the game, but he'd seen screen captures. Sleek, dark leather armour. It was an almost stereotypical roguish style. He thought he had the skills to handle the design she wanted.

"Took you long enough," Niall grumbled when he opened the door again.

"Coffee," Dannel repeated. He stepped out of the flat, rolling his foot slightly to get his trainer on properly. "Who are you?"

"Niall Bishop."

"Yes, but who are you?" Dannel wanted more than a name.

"Travel vlogger." Niall followed him down the stairs. "Photographer. Run a YouTube channel all about hiking on a budget."

On a budget.

The few times Niall had been around, he'd worn nothing but high-end clothing. He wore shoes Dannel had seen one of the solicitors at Wayne's office have. Expensive ones. They probably cost more than his paycheck as a firefighter.

"Did your mum and dad leave you money?" Dannel couldn't stop the question. "I can't imagine travel vlogs make enough money for swanky shoes or the gear required for hiking. Archie saved up for ages to kit himself out for a year of travel."

"My grandfather, actually. Not that it's any of your business." Niall exited the building behind him. "Where are we going? You haven't answered my question."

Dannel pointed down the street to the café on the corner. "We can get a coffee. I'm no good in the mornings without a kick of caffeine. I don't remember your question."

"Fine." Niall sighed rather dramatically. "What did you say to Archie last night? I saw you and your boyfriend chatting with him once I left."

"I didn't say anything," he replied honestly. Osian had done most of the talking. "Do you love Archie?"

"Do I…." Niall trailed off, shaking his head. "Is this a 'don't hurt my friend' sort of lecture? Aren't we too old to be beating our chests?"

"No." Dannel was confused. Did anyone ever get too old for their friends to show concern? "I didn't beat my chest. Why would I hurt myself?"

"Are you being funny?"

"Not on purpose." Dannel stepped up to the counter, ignoring Niall's sputtering.

Ordering his usual coffee, sausage roll, and choco-late croissant, Dannel made his way outside to an empty table. He'd barely taken a bite when Niall joined him. The awkward silence lingered between them.

Dannel grew tired of pretending they were eating on their own. He didn't want to spend his entire morning dancing around the topic. "Did you snog some bloke outside the theatre?"

"Excuse me?"

"Did you snog—"

"I heard you." Niall cut him off with an irritated wave of his hand. "Not sure I appreciate being accused of cheating."

"Do you ever answer questions directly?" Dannel might as well go for his run now, even after eating breakfast, if Niall had no intentions of genuinely responding. "Birdie saw you snogging some bloke."

"And?"

Is that neurotypical for yes?

Dannel finished his sausage roll while contemplating Niall's blasé attitude. "Is yours an open relationship?"

"None of your business."

"So, no then." Dannel folded the top of the bag on his chocolate croissant. He'd save it for later. "Is Archie aware?"

"What do you think we were arguing about last night?"

You murdering his mum? Was Archie lying last night or is Niall doing so now? Or did you argue about both?

"This is a waste of time." Niall shoved away from the table. He grabbed his coffee so roughly that it sloshed out of the top. "Damn it."

"He stomps off a lot." Dannel watched Niall leave with a slight feeling of confusion.

What have I learnt? Niall definitely cheated on Archie. Birdie likely confronted him about it. Does it make him a killer?

Probably.

As Haider would say, he's got motive.

Handing his untouched croissant and coffee to one of the rough sleepers in the park, Dannel took off at a slow jog. He knew many of them by name. They generally tended to refuse help aside from the occasional meal.

Dannel jogged a meandering loop through the park and returned to the flat. He slipped into the shop on the ground floor, waving to his auntie behind the counter. "Morning."

"You've missed your uncle. He's gone to move furniture for your mum." Auntie Myriam held her arms out for a hug. She always waited to see if he wanted one. "I've missed you, sweetheart. Are you and your Ossie doing well? Enjoying the change of pace? Not missing running into burning buildings."

"We're all right." Dannel helped her empty several boxes and stock shelves with a variety of Jamaican spices. The shop sold all sorts of difficult to find products from throughout the Caribbean. "I miss my friends. The chief. Some nights I miss the excitement. And the thrill of knowing I've helped save a life."

"But?"

"I remember the barrage of sound from the sirens and the flashing lights. The assault on my senses every night. I can feel the intensity of struggling to not hit sensory overload every shift." Dannel knew deep within himself the decision to leave the station had been the right one. "I couldn't handle the stress much longer without breaking down."

She reached up to kiss him on the cheek. "I'm so proud of you, love. Your uncle and I both are."

Dannel shuffled uneasily and returned his attention to organising the broad selection of curry powders. "Are there any other boxes?"

She pinched his cheek, chuckling, and pointing to a stack behind the counter. "Just like your uncle. Never able to take a compliment for anything."

Working in the empty shop was almost meditative in nature. Dannel rearranged the shelves while stocking them. He spent an hour, putting everything in order.

His uncle and auntie had gone out of their way to make the shop a Caribbean pantry oasis. It smelled of sweets and spices. The shelves were packed with a variety of goods imported from Jamaica, Barbados, Dominica, and a host of other islands.

Some weeks, his auntie Myriam also sold home-baked gizzada, a tart filled with sweet and spiced coconut. It was one of his favourite childhood sweets.

"Why don't you take this upstairs and have coffee with cake?" Myriam brought him out of his alphabetizing of various brands of crisps. "Off with you. I'll be opening the shop soon, and you won't feel quite so relaxed."

Spiced coconut cake, coffee, and working on a new cosplay design.

Not a bad way to spend the rest of his day until Osian came home.

THIRTEEN

OSIAN

Breakfast with his mum and dad had gone by quickly. Osian decided to check on Ian at the theatre. He knew the camera hadn't captured anything interesting so far.

Chris kept telling them to be patient. *Patience is a virtue. Says everyone who isn't required to wait.*

While he was on the tube, Dannel texted him about the strange encounter with Niall. *Intriguing development.* Osian wondered what the man had hoped to gain from confronting them.

It hadn't made them any less suspicious of him.

They texted about Niall and Archie. He also mentioned his auntie Myriam's weird fetish of hoarding boxes of orange jelly for no reason since no one bought them at the store. Osian had just enough time to offer a few suggestions on Dannel's initial sketch before arriving at his stop.

Osian was greeted outside the Evelyn Lavelle by what appeared to be the entire ensemble. "Something wrong?"

"He's panicking in his dressing room." Hope, one of the principal dancers in the ensemble, gestured toward the theatre. "One of our principles was almost electrocuted in the loo earlier when live wiring dropped in front of him. Have you met Derrick? His parents are part of the—"

"My parents don't matter. And we don't actually know what happened," Derrick, another one of the other dancers, corrected. "We don't even know if Edwin is seriously injured. He's dramatic at the best of times."

"He's not seriously injured. I heard he'd scarpered from the hospital the second the paramedics dropped him off," Hope interjected.

Deciding not to make a joke about what an electrifying performance it must've been, Osian went to check on Ian. He grabbed his phone to text Chris and Abra to see if she could find out who'd dropped Edwin at the hospital. The cameras might've caught something, depending on if the loo was backstage or the ones upfront.

Chris: Don't go in the loo.

Don't go in the loo?

I'm not daft. I wouldn't investigate and get myself elec-trocuted. Who am I kidding? I definitely would.

Ian first, though.

Osian found Ian panicking while two incredibly familiar detectives tried to ask him questions. He was surprised they'd been called out. "Hello, Detective Inspector squared. Isn't an electrical accident below your pay grade?"

"I suppose I shouldn't be surprised to see you here." Haider shared a glance with his partner, who rolled her eyes. "Try to resist the urge to investigate. And don't go switching any lights on or off until we figure out what happened."

"Pardon?" Osian frowned in confusion.

"One of the light switches must have been wired wrong. It caused a short when it was turned on," Ian answered with his face still buried in a scarf.

"With a shock to one of your actors?" Osian asked when Ian failed to continue. He glanced over at Haider, who was shaking his head. "You don't think so?"

"I'm not going to jump to any conclusions."

Ian lifted his head up from the scarf. "My show.

My beautiful show. What am I going to do? Murders. Electrocutions. Ghosts."

Osian eased between the detectives and crouched in front of Ian. "You're too fabulous to give up."

"You're a sweet lad." Ian patted him on the head. "I'll never forgive myself if someone else is hurt."

"Mr Garey. If you wouldn't mind?" Detective Inspector Powell nodded toward the door. "We'd like to wrap up our questions and determine what exactly has happened."

Osian squeezed Ian's hand and got to his feet. "I'll hang around for a while. You'll be all right. The show must go on, after all."

Leaving Ian with the police, Osian stepped out into the hallway. He considered eavesdropping, until Haider poked his head out of the dressing room and suggested he jog on. *Rude. It's almost as if he doesn't trust me.*

It didn't take long to find the right loo. Police tape once again blocked off a doorway at the Evelyn Lavelle. An Out of Order sign hung on it as an extra warning.

Osian stepped under the caution tape to investigate. "Looks perfectly normal."

What does a damaged light switch look like?

He knew little about the electrical wiring. It was hard to believe someone could actually pull off such a heinous prank. *Or was the joke actually a feigned electrocution? Did the actor fake the accident?*

If so, why? To draw attention to the show? Poor Birdie's murder already brought a level of infamy to it.

Sending a follow-up message to Chris, Osian wished he'd brought his laptop. He could check the footage for himself. They had a camera pointed down the hallway, which would've captured anyone going in or out of the loo.

The buzz of his mobile caught his attention. Chris hadn't seen anyone entering the bathroom aside from the actor who was injured. He texted over a short clip of footage.

He's quite literally the worst actor I've ever seen.

Or the best?

No, worst.

How had anyone bought the story of him being electrocuted? The actor had stepped out of the bathroom and glanced around before shouting and swooning dramatically to the floor. He managed to land gently on the carpet.

A second message arrived from Abra. She hadn't been on duty but one of their friends had.

The supposedly electrocuted actor had vanished from the hospital.

"Do you ever listen?" Haider had obviously finished with Ian. "I knew you'd be in here."

"Watch." Osian reached out toward the light switch.

"What are you—" Haider lunged for him a second too late. Osian had flicked the switch and nothing happened. "Have you lost your mind?"

"You don't find it strange this actor suddenly claimed to have been electrocuted, made a massive deal about a murder attempt, only to vanish the second he arrived at the hospital according to one of my mates?" Osian refused to acknowledge the slow ebb of adrenaline and his lowering blood pressure. "For whatever reason, he faked his accident."

"We're going to talk about this." Haider gestured to the light switch. "You and your complete lack of care over your own well-being. Long, long conversations until you stop running on impulse."

"It was a safe guess." Osian tried to defend his decision, ignoring the cynically raised eyebrow of the detective. "Did Chris send you the video? I asked him to."

"Not yet." Haider held a hand up, pausing to

speak into his radio to have a constable track down the injured actor. "And we're also going to discuss those cameras you put up in my crime scene."

"Okay, first, you released the crime scene. And we had the owner's permission to add a second layer of security to the Evelyn Lavelle theatre, practically a national treasure." Osian smiled winningly at the detective while lying through his teeth. They'd gotten Ian's permission, and he definitely wasn't the owner. "I swear, I was certain the accident had been faked. And badly."

"Be more careful." Haider sighed very deeply. "And you could've just showed me the video."

"Yes, Mum. I could've, but where would the fun in that be?" Osian sensed an impending lecture coming from the detective. He decided to make a quick exit. "I'll be going now. I'm sure Dannel's at home waiting for me. Give us a call if you find anything."

He wouldn't. Osian knew Haider wanted them far away from the investigation. He ducked out of the theatre, avoiding Detective Inspector Powell who still stood sentry by Ian's dressing room.

And once again, I'm left with more questions than answers.

The walk home gave Osian time to process his

thoughts over the morning's adventure. He wondered if Edwin was behind the ghostly presence at the Evelyn Lavelle. Had the actor grown tired of simple tricks and moved on to something more dramatic?

Why else would someone fake getting injured in such a dramatic fashion?

Could he be trying to take attention away from Birdie's murder?

Maybe we should spend more time looking through the footage from our nanny cams and watch more closely over the next few days.

Who knows what we might see?

FOURTEEN

DANNEL

DANNEL STARED BLANKLY AT HIS OVER-EXCITED boyfriend. He held a hand up, waiting for Osian to stop verbally vomiting all over him. "We've clearly been attached at the hip for way too long. You're starting to ramble like I do."

"Electrocuted," Osian practically shouted the word. "Did you miss that point?"

"Inside voice." Dannel couldn't help chuckling at the sudden swap. "Have we switched bodies? Maybe try speaking slowly so I can understand what you said?"

"You're not funny."

"I'm hilarious."

"Electrocuted," Osian reiterated.

"Except he wasn't. And neither were you."

Dannel continued perusing the contents of the fridge, trying to find something appealing to snack on. "Think Haider's caught up to him? The actor? What was his name?"

"Edwin something or other. I don't remember his surname. Doesn't matter, I suppose." Osian squeezed in next to him and reached in to grab a container of leftover pasta. "Want to split this with me? Too late for lunch and too early for dinner?"

"All right."

"We should stake out the theatre." Osian pointed to the laptop on the counter. "From home. We can have snacks, coffee, and cake. Stay up late, watching the most boring show in London."

"For what?"

"Ghosts? Murderers? Naughty people snogging in hallways?"

Dannel figured spying from home was safer than camping out at the Evelyn Lavelle. "Do you think Edwin could be Birdie's killer?"

"Maybe."

Neither of them knew the answer for sure. Edwin didn't seem to have a real motive. Then again, why had he faked being shocked by faulty wiring?

"Why don't we pepper Ian with questions about

his theatre company? Everyone from the principles to the ensemble to the orchestra to the tea lady." Dannel grabbed the laptop and carried it over to the sofa. "He can tell us who Edwin would share his secrets with. Can you see him keeping this a secret?"

"Murder or a prank?"

"Prank." Dannel thought Edwin might be responsible for the fake ghost. He didn't see a reason for the actor to have killed Birdie. "We might actually solve Ian's paranormal mystery."

Osian hopped over the back of the couch and flopped onto a cushion beside Dannel. "We'll make a list of questions. Ask everyone the same ones. See what we find out. Who knows? We could solve the murder as well."

"Text Ian. He can bully everyone into showing up early for rehearsals." Dannel hoped they'd be more open to chatting with them than they'd been with the police. "What about Niall? Still think he might've done it. Got questions for him."

"And Archie."

"And Archie," Dannel agreed.

They watched the live feed from the security cameras on their laptop in silence. Osian periodi-cally texted with Ian about their plan for the morning while Dannel focused on coming up with a list of questions. He hoped it would help organise their thoughts.

We should jot down the times the ghost appeared, then attempt to corroborate where each member of the company was.

What else?

Probably best to avoid any questions that are too obvious. They're not going to come right out and say, oh, it was me, are they? Not likely.

"Ian's hired a new costume designer." Osian tossed his phone onto the coffee table. He bent forward to see the list of questions. "We should ask how they got on with Birdie and if they had any issues with Ian. And see if they have any thoughts on who's behind the ghost and the murder."

"Why with Ian?" Dannel found it hard to imagine anyone disliking their elderly neighbour. "Everyone adores him."

"True. Doesn't it seem like someone genuinely wants to ruin his play?" Osian twisted around to rest his head in Dannel's lap with his feet propped up on the arm of the sofa. "The only other option is someone's trying to turn the company into a spectacle to entice people to show up."

"Or they're simply a complete and utter prat."

"I don't think they're mutually exclusive. A wanker trying to ruin Ian's play or an attention-seeking prat who wants to draw in a larger audience." Osian tilted his head to watch the laptop. "Not sure which is worse."

"What about the new costume designer?" Dannel dropped his fingers down to scratch Osian's head gently. "Maybe they wanted Birdie's job?"

"Doubtful." Osian stretched contentedly, shifting on the sofa to get more comfortable. "Ian claims he stole them from another production."

"Stole's probably an exaggeration."

"It is Ian." Osian grinned up at Dannel. "Ian eats drama with his tea."

"Sounds crunchy." Dannel returned his gaze to the cameras. "If he hired them over from another project, they wouldn't need to kill Birdie for the job. They already had one."

"They might've."

"Occam's Razor."

"What?"

"The simplest explanation quite often tends to be correct," Dannel paraphrased. "You don't off someone to get their job when you've already got one. Ian's not paying more than one of the larger production companies in the city. He's barely cobbled together his play as it is."

"Did you see?" Osian rolled onto his side to get a closer view of the laptop. He pointed to the top right square, one from the camera angled down the stairs leading to the basement. "A black shadow."

"Ossie."

"I saw something."

They watched in tense silence. Nothing. Dannel opened his mouth to speak then immediately stopped when a dark image flitted down the stairs. A second later, the camera flickered before freezing.

"How…." Osian didn't seem to know what question he wanted to ask.

"Technology isn't foolproof." Dannel knew enough to know any security system had the potential to fail or be hacked. "All the cameras froze. Maintenance?"

"Worst. Timing. Ever."

"We've seen enough true crime shows to know security cameras aren't a guarantee for any investigation." Dannel watched Osian get up and straighten his clothes. "Ossie."

"Aren't you a little curious?"

Well, yes.

"That's beside the point."

Osian grinned suddenly at him. "We can pick up a double pepperoni and spicy honey and a 'nduja one from Pizza Pilgrims. Maybe get two Nutella rings as well. Plus a couple cold beers."

THE 'NDUJA PIZZA WAS ONE OF DANNEL'S favourites. Spicy sausage on an oven-fired pie. He'd smash a whole one on his own, plus dessert. They both enjoyed the ring of dough filled with chocolate spread and salted ricotta.

"Right. So, ghosts, then stuff ourselves with pizza. Sounds like a great way to end the day." Dannel shot off the couch. He caught his trainers when Osian tossed them to him one at a time. "Should we text Chris?"

"After. We don't know anything yet."

This is a terrible idea.

Absolutely stupid.

"He'll figure it out." Dannel had no doubts Chris kept an eye on the cameras whenever possible. "Why don't we walk to the theatre? Ian might still be there. It's only mid-afternoon. We can meet the new costume designer at the very least."

Safety in numbers.

They grabbed coffees and made their way to

the theatre. Rain had cooled the temperature off slightly. It made a pleasant walk; Dannel could almost pretend they were on a date except for the growing sense of impending doom in the pit of his stomach.

"Ossie." Dannel grabbed Osian's arm, stopping him before he crossed the street. "Haider."

The entire theatre company stood outside the Evelyn Lavelle. Several marked police cars were parked outside, along with a vehicle Dannel recognised as Haider's. Something had obviously happened.

"Well, that's not good," Osian uttered the understatement of the century when they spotted a crime scene investigators van pull up. "You don't think someone else has been murdered?"

I think we should've stayed home eating leftover pasta.

I also think we're not getting our pizza anytime soon.

"Given the ambulance is pulling away without taking anyone away, I do." Dannel nodded toward the vehicle driving off into traffic. "What the hell is happening at the Evelyn Lavelle?"

"Murder."

"Prat." Dannel flicked him on the arm. "The good news is we can't possibly be responsible for whatever's happened."

The bad news is something's obviously gone wrong. Again.

They jogged across the street, dodging a slowly moving lorry who'd obviously been watching the excitement at the theatre. They snuck by Haider, who was in deep conversation with Detective Inspector Powell. Dannel was surprised the police didn't notice them blending in with the rest of the company.

"Hello, you two," Hope whispered. "Ian's inside."

"Inside?" Dannel's heart froze in his chest. He tried not to immediately assume the worst. "Why?"

"We're not sure." Hope was in a huddle with several other members of the ensemble, their arms wrapped around one another for comfort. "The power seemed to flicker briefly. We heard a scream. Next thing we knew, the coppers were rushing us all out here. Said not to leave. Colin heard them talking about another body being found."

"Ian?" Osian asked the question Dannel couldn't quite manage to voice.

Colin lifted his head off Hope's shoulder. "I'm not sure. I don't think so. I heard Ian's voice, so he's fine unless they managed to perform a séance and he spoke from the afterlife."

Osian leaned closer to Dannel when he grabbed his hand. "Haider's not calling any spirits back from the dead."

"If you want to sneak inside, we can cause a diversion." Hope pointed to where the coroners could be seen dealing with a body bag on a stretcher. "Ian would appreciate the support. Or smelling salts."

"Smelling salts aren't pleasant." Dannel didn't think the high-strung Ian needed to be hyped up by a sniff of ammonia inhalant. "What sort of distraction?"

"An impromptu rehearsal on the street?"

"Juggling." Colin pulled several balls out of his pockets. "Takes a lot of work to pretend to be dreadful at it."

"Takes a lot of effort to pretend to be dreadful at just about anything when you're brilliant." Hope winked at Dannel before pushing him and Osian in the direction of the door. "Go on. Solve our mystery for us."

"I'm beginning to think instead of a cosplay business and a podcast, we should've become private investigators, since everyone already assumes we are." Osian tried to walk normally while also hiding behind the cast. "We look ridiculous."

"Pretty sure actual private investigators sneak quietly." Dannel was trying and failing not to laugh. "You're drawing more attention trying to squash yourself into a short person."

"No sense of adventure."

In the chaos of the entire ensemble demonstrating their party tricks to the confused detectives, Osian and Dannel slipped into the building. He almost felt sorry for Haider. No one excelled at creating distractions more than bored theatre performers.

Skirting the crime scene technicians chatting in the corner of the lobby, Osian followed Dannel through the doors into the passageway down to Ian's sanctuary. He was draped across the chaise lounge. One of the actors stood beside him, using a program to fan his face.

"Oh, darlings," Ian greeted them with a tired wave. "Have you heard our terrible news?"

Osian sat on the edge of the desk, leaving the chair for Dannel. "We saw the police. Did they find something?"

"Someone." Ian sat up slowly. He seemed to have aged ten years since Dannel had last seen him.

His hand gripped on to his fellow actor. "Howard Osman. One of our assistant designers. A young, talented costumer. I found him at the bottom of the stairs leading to the storage room."

Bugger.

We're going to need a completely different set of questions.

"Have the police said anything?" Osian pulled out his phone and began to make notes. Dannel could see he was jotting down additional questions at the end of the list they'd made earlier. *Great minds.* "About Howard?"

"Nothing. They ordered everyone outside. Left me here." Ian clutched his hands together. "What if they believe I murdered the poor darling?"

"You?" Dannel couldn't think of anyone less likely to commit murder than Ian. "I'm sure they're only interested in making sure they get a clear witness statement from you."

"Mr Barrett? We're ready—" Haider stopped mid-sentence, glancing around the room with an air of resigned annoyance. "Could you two stay out of my case for five seconds?"

"The argument could be made that we were out of your case all day." Osian ignored Dannel's persistent poking to his side. "We didn't know anything had happened."

Haider brought a hand up to rub his forehead.

"Listen—"

"No." Haider cut Osian off while continuing to massage his forehead with his eyes closed. "I'm going to need Mr Barrett to come down to speak with us about what he saw. And I'm going to need *you* to not get involved."

"Polite way of saying sod off, you nosy bastards." Osian grinned while reaching into his pocket for his phone. Dannel leaned forward to see him sending a quick text to Chris about the cameras and a second to their friendly solicitor, Wayne. "I wonder if we'll get a commission from Wayne for all the work we've sent his way."

"Maybe he'll send us a fruit basket." Dannel wondered if Haider was going to lose his temper. "Isn't that what fancy law offices do?"

"If you're finished?" Haider had obviously decided to pretend they weren't there. He motioned for Ian to follow. "Your friend can come with you."

Osian stood up.

"Not you. The silent, helpful one with the fan." Haider stepped out of the room, waiting for Ian to join him. His attention returned to Dannel and Osian. "Please go home."

They watched the three leave. Dannel stared at the closed door. Osian was busy on his phone, responding to text messages.

"Are we going home?" Dannel asked.

"Not bloody likely. Chris is on his way. He wants to inspect the cameras. Why don't I chat with the company? They're probably all milling around outside the theatre." Osian rested his head against Dannel's arm briefly. "See if you can find anything in Ian's room or in Birdie's old one. We'll wait for reinforcements before tackling the storage room again."

Well, we're knee-deep in the mystery.

What's a little more investigating going to do?

FIFTEEN
OSIAN

Osian had left Dannel to snoop around in Ian's room while he went outside to speak to the company. "Poor Ian. His play's turning into more of a tragedy than anything else."

Will they have to cancel the play?

Most of the cast had dispersed when Osian got outside. Hope and her friend Colin stood nearby, a little ways away from the entrance. They were having a heated, whispered conversation with someone he couldn't see.

Osian walked toward them and realised immediately who they were chatting with. "Archie?"

His friend paled considerably, then jogged off across the street without a word. Osian considered chasing after him, but Archie had a head start. He decided to stay and interrogate the two actors instead.

"Do you know Archie well?" Osian didn't want them running off. "Through Birdie?"

"Not incredibly well. Birdie talked about him loads, though." Hope and Colin exchanged uncomfortable glances with one another. "We should go. We've got rehearsals in the morning."

"Hang on." Osian held out a hand, stopping short of actually grabbing either of them. "What were you arguing about?"

"You know his boyfriend?" Hope asked. She waited for Osian to nod and continued. "Niall was at the theatre around noon. He's been seeing one of the dancers in the ensemble."

"Has he?" Osian momentarily forgot about Archie's sudden disappearance. "Which one?"

"Daisy."

"And Michael," Colin added. He nodded when Hope spun toward him. "I saw them snogging in the stairwell."

"Cheeky fellow." Hope shook her head. "He's handsome enough. Seeing two people in a company's risky if everyone's not aware."

"Considering he's got a boyfriend." Colin seemed to agree with her. "Daisy claimed she's known him since primary school, though. They grew up together."

"Explains why he was hanging around without Archie." Hope tucked her hands into her pockets. "I wondered why he kept showing up during rehearsals."

Well, well, well, Birdie definitely saw Niall cheating on Archie.

"Is that what you were telling Archie about?" Osian figured learning your boyfriend had cheated on you multiple times might definitely lead to a heated conversation. "Niall's cheating?"

"Not at first." Colin began to absently toss several balls in the air, juggling with an impressive amount of ease. "He asked about the hoopla at the theatre first. Then I accidentally mentioned seeing Niall."

"Accidentally?" Hope scoffed. "We've been trying to figure out a way to warn him. It was just so awkward."

"When did Niall leave?" Osian wondered if he'd been in the theatre when Howard was pushed down the stairs.

"I've no idea. I never saw him leave." Hope snatched one of Colin's balls out of the air. "Listen, we've got to run. We have an audition later."

Once the actors had left, Osian tracked Dannel down inside the theatre. They decided to wait for Chris. The creepy stairs bothered them too much to enter without reinforcements.

And Haider thinks we take too many dangerous risks.

Osian wandered down the aisle to find Dannel seated in the front row. He dropped into a chair next to him and shared what he'd learned. "So, Niall was cheating."

"Message Archie." Dannel nudged his knee. "See what he's got to say. Maybe he didn't see you."

"He saw me. I doubt he'll answer, but why not." Osian imagined Archie knew they'd have questions for him. "He has to have seen me. Why else did he suddenly run off?"

There was no response to his text to Archie. Osian didn't even get the annoying dots, showing the message had been received. What was going on with him?

Had Archie suddenly realised his mum was right?

And regrets killing her?

Or is he wondering if Niall lied about his involvement with Birdie's death?

Stretching his legs out, Osian thought sitting in the empty theatre was serene. The sounds of plays past seemed to linger in the air. He could under-stand why lights were left on for the ghosts.

The theatre felt alive even without anyone rehearsing. There was no music. Yet, Osian thought a strange rhythm vibrated in the air.

Okay. Maybe it's time we went to grab our pizza. I'm clearly reading too much into this.

They weren't completely alone in the theatre. Several members of the lighting department had remained once the police allowed them in to continue their work. The play was scheduled for a preview in less than a week.

Will it even make opening night if people keep dying?

"I spoke to one of the crime scene techs who were in Ian's room. They didn't find anything in the basement." Dannel slouched further down into the seat. "Ever notice how lovely the seats in the Evelyn Lavelle are?"

"Quality from a different age." Osian fumbled in his pocket when his phone buzzed. He finally got it out. "Chris is waiting outside for us."

"They can't genuinely believe Ian shoved someone down the stairs, can they?" Dannel dragged himself up out of the seat. "I mean, it's Ian."

"I doubt it." Osian worried about their elderly

neighbour. "I haven't heard anything from Wayne or Ian."

"You promised me pizza," Dannel complained absently.

"I'm peckish as well. Why don't we see if we can talk Chris into going with us? He might even pay." Osian figured if they invited Abra, he wouldn't be able to say no. "We'll let him work up an appetite first, though, poking around at the cameras."

"You have sneaky looks on your faces." Chris greeted them with narrowed eyes and a suspicious glare. "The answer is no."

"Rude." Osian grinned innocently which didn't improve matters. "Which cameras do you want to check out first?"

"They're back up and running." Chris apparently decided to let matters rest and focus on the job at hand. "My educated guess is someone used a stronger signal on the same frequency to jam the signal. The downside to using a wireless system."

"Could it be an accident?" Dannel was ever the optimist.

"Maybe. You said the power flickered? It's possible that caused the problem." Chris didn't sound convinced. "I'm most interested in the camera by the stairs. You said someone was pushed down them?"

"One of the costumers brought up to help redo the costumes. Just an assistant." Osian wondered whether the two murders were connected to the play, the costume department specifically, or Niall's cheating. Had Howard been another one of his snogging partners? "What can you learn from the camera?"

"I want to make sure no one messed with them."

While Chris inspected the cameras with Dannel's help, Osian continued on down the stairs. He pulled the door to the storage room open, peering inside. Nothing had been disturbed from the last time they were there.

No new speaker hiding to terrify them.

"Osian," Chris called out a warning to him. "Oz. Try not to get your fingerprints all over everything."

"Keep your shirt on. I'm not touching anything." Osian frowned at a scrap of fabric sticking out from under several stacked backdrops. "I'll be out in a second."

Where have I seen that before?

"Osian."

Osian ignored Chris and went deeper into the room, crouching down beside the thick cloth backdrops to get a closer look at what appeared to be part of a shirt sleeve. When he tugged on it, a limp arm flopped out. "Oh. Bollocks."

"Osian?" Dannel sounded worried. "What's wrong?"

Osian had to clear his throat a few times. He fell backwards away from what he knew would be a body. "You need to call Haider."

"Why?" Chris asked.

"Ossie?" Dannel poked his head into the room.

"They missed a body."

"I could be having pizza right now." Dannel shifted uncomfortably in the chair. He stared across the auditorium to where Osian sat. "Warm, cheesy, delicious slices of Italian brilliance."

The police had arrived quite quickly when Chris called and hadn't been pleased or surprised to find Osian and Dannel in the middle of their investigation. Then again, who expected to find a body in the basement?

Anyone who's ever watched a true crime show on the telly?

Or listened to our podcast?

After cordoning off the stairs for the second time, Haider had separated the three of them in the auditorium. Chris sat near the stage, Osian lorded it up in one of the boxes, and Dannel slumped into the back row near the exit. Far enough from each other talking wasn't going to be an issue.

He hadn't thought to remove their phones, so it didn't take long for them to join a group chat.

Osian: In retrospect, getting pizza first would've been a wise decision.

Dannel: Think Haider will let us order in? Bet we could get some delivered. I'm starving.

Chris: We found a dead body. Could you two try to focus?

Osian: Yeah, Bond, I'm fully aware. My stomach isn't.

Chris: I'm not James Bond.

Osian: If the shoe fits.

Dannel: Is he the same size as Daniel Craig?

Osian: Not the point.

"What part of don't talk amongst yourself did you miss?" Haider stepped into the auditorium from the exit by the stage. "I can hear you muttering up there, Garey. Don't protest your innocence. You're like teenagers sent to sit outside the headmistress's office, whispering amongst yourselves. Quit sending notes."

"No whispering was involved," Dannel insisted.

"Typing, then."

With a roll of his eyes, Haider waved them all over. Osian disappeared through the door of his box and reappeared a minute later behind the detective. They followed Haider down the hall through to the lobby.

"I'm heading to the station. Can I give you a lift?"

"Polite yet firm way of saying we're about to be interrogated." Osian draped an arm across Dannel's shoulders. "So, who was the poor sod under the flats?"

"Flats?"

"Stage backdrops," Dannel answered Haider's question.

Haider glanced between the three men. He seemed to consider his answer for a moment. "Niall Bishop."

Dannel started in surprise. He exchanged a look with Osian, who appeared equally shocked. "Niall?"

Is this why Archie was at the theatre?

Without even asking, Dannel knew Osian was considering the same thought. Archie had run off when Osian spotted him. Had there been a more sinister reason for his presence at the Evelyn Lavelle?

Something odd was definitely going on at the theatre. Three murders. Seemingly unconnected. Plus a ghost. Was it all the same person?

Had Niall killed Birdie?

"I haven't killed anyone."

Dannel tuned back in to the conversation as Osian's voice rose. "What?"

"This numpty asked if we had anything to do with it." Osian folded his arms across his chest, glowering at the detective.

"Standard questions I've got to ask everyone," Haider insisted. "Please don't make this more difficult."

Difficult, when Osian was his regular self, was the default setting. Dannel didn't think Haider would find that comforting. He'd initially met Osian when he'd been at the start of recovering from traumatic events.

Healing does take time.

Dannel had wondered for a while if Osian would ever fully return to himself, the jovial, teasing man who'd laughed his way through life while caring deeply about those around him. "Ossie didn't murder anyone."

"We're aware." Detective Inspector Powell joined them. "It would make our lives so much easier if you weren't the ones showing up with the dead bodies all the time."

"I didn't stumble on Niall on purpose," Osian protested indignantly. "We're not trying to complicate the investigation."

After a long lecture on avoiding crime scenes in the future, the detectives let them go. Chris invited them to his place. Dannel knew they all wanted to discuss what had happened. They picked up pizzas on the way over, six of them plus Nutella rings and beer.

"What a day." Chris sat on his leather armchair, waving them at the couch. He grabbed one of the boxes of pizza and a beer. "How do you two keep finding these bizarre mysteries?"

"Three bodies and a ghost." Osian shuffled through the boxes to find one of the pepperoni ones. "Sounds like a Netflix movie."

"Starring Samuel L. Jackson as the ghost." Dannel popped the cap of his beer using the edge of the table, earning a glare from Chris. "I'd watch it."

"You'd cosplay as the ghost." Osian grabbed a slice of pizza, using the box as a plate. "The question I have is whether or not Archie knew Niall was dead."

"Knew he was dead?" Dannel wondered if their gentle ginger giant had fooled all of them. Was he capable of murdering his boyfriend? And his mother? "Or killed him?"

"Did you notice anything out of the ordinary in the basement?" Chris wiped pizza sauce from his face and grabbed his bottle of beer.

"Other than the lifeless hand? No." Osian set his pizza down on the coffee table. "What about the cameras? Did they catch it?"

"Motion capture cameras aren't perfect." Chris went for a second slice of pizza. "We used them in the hopes anytime someone entered the stairwell, it'd trigger them. So either someone purposefully disrupted the Wi-Fi signal or messed with the camera itself."

"Or the camera failed on its own." Dannel knew no matter how expensive the technology; nothing was perfect. "Maybe this is why the police still do stakeouts instead of solely relying on CCTV footage."

"So, what are you going to do now?" Chris prompted after several minutes of silent eating. "Find Archie?"

Osian glanced over at Dannel. "Smash this pizza, check in on Ian since Haider wouldn't say how he's doing, and see how Archie responds to Niall's death."

"And I'll see if the cameras were a complete fail or if there's something on them."

"We're so glad you used this murder investigation for untested equipment." Osian saluted Chris with his beer.

"Ossie." Dannel couldn't tell if Osian was being serious or teasing. Chris was laughing, so he assumed it had been a joke. "Why don't I help with the footage? I can watch while I'm working on my new costume commission."

"Sure. Leave me the hard part of trying to get Ian to speak sense. You know he's going to be flailing dramatically." Osian shoved his pizza box to the side and grabbed for one of the Nutella rings. "I'm going to need something to sustain me."

"Or put you to sleep." Dannel was already feeling the start of a food coma. "How much pizza is too much?"

"No such thing. Don't be daft." Osian managed to fit an entire slice of the chocolate-hazelnut pizza ring into his mouth. "I might be sick."

By the time they got home, Dannel felt like the

day had been three centuries long. He grabbed his earbuds, stripped out of his clothes, and collapsed on the bed with a groan. Osian simply opened the windows to allow some fresh air into the stuffy flat and let him bleed off the day listening to music.

I love how he never tries to make me fit into a non-autistic box.

SEVENTEEN
OSIAN

T̲HE FOLLOWING MORNING, O̲SIAN KNEW immediately Dannel had pushed himself too hard over the last few days. He had a tendency to ignore the signs of overload. Sleeping in had been the first sign.

Dannel didn't sleep in when the smell of coffee filled the flat.

"Why don't I let you have the flat to yourself? I want to track down Archie." Osian set a mug of tea and a plate of leftover pizza on the nightstand.

Getting ready to go out, Osian exited the bathroom to find Dannel had trudged across to his workspace. He was singing along to "Wait For It" from the *Hamilton* cast album, pizza and coffee on the desk far away from his sketchbook. *Right. He's sorted for the day.*

Osian went into the room, pressing a kiss to the top of Dannel's head. "I'll be back later."

Not taking the silence personally, Osian returned to the bedroom. He changed into jeans and a comfortable T-shirt. Despite rain the day before, the weather was still absolutely boiling.

Okay.

What do I need to do? Track down Archie, see what he knows about Niall's death. If he knows about it. Head to the theatre and make sure Ian's not stressing himself into a heart attack.

"I love you."

Osian chuckled at the shout coming from further into the apartment. "Love you too."

No matter how stressed out, Dannel had a habit of never leaving or having Osian go without saying "I love you." *What if one of us dies? What if our last words to each other are something absolutely stupid like "don't forget to clean the toilet?"*

He had a point.

"Osian? Darling?" Ian poked his head out of his flat when Osian jogged down the stairs. "Can you come inside?"

"Are you all right?" Osian skidded to a halt and

retracted the last few steps. Ian seemed more a wilted flower than his bright, sprightly self. "No rehearsals this morning?"

"Postponed." Ian wrapped his lush dressing robe around him more tightly. "Care for an espresso?"

"Never say no to coffee." Osian followed him into the kitchen, where Ian carefully poured him a drink in one of his tiny, perfect cups. "You didn't answer my question, though. Are you okay? Did the detective inspectors rough you up?"

"You're very sweet, darling. I'm perfectly fine." Ian lowered himself into an armchair in the living room, reaching over to reduce the volume on the radio. "Young Haider was quite gentlemanly; even gave me a lift home."

"Another conquest?" Osian grinned.

"A gentleman never kisses and tells, darling." Ian sipped his espresso delicately. "They did mention when they returned after rushing out to the theatre that another body had been found."

"Oh?" Osian hoped Haider had been more forthcoming to Ian.

"Yes, left me there at the police station. Languishing on my own."

"I'll bet my last slice of pizza you had the

constables wrapped around your fingers in no time at all." Osian wasn't buying the "woe is me" act from the man. "Am I wrong?"

"I've no idea what you're referring to. It's perfectly natural for them to bring tea and pastries from the café around the corner." Ian adjusted his robe slightly, brushing off a stray hair from his arm. "He only asked if I had been aware of Niall Bishop's presence at the theatre. I wasn't. My morning was spent on the stage, finalising the details of a tricky part of the first act."

Osian sipped the overly strong coffee, trying not to make faces at the bitter taste. "Be careful when you're at the theatre."

"I am always careful, darling."

Careful might not be enough.

They chatted for several minutes. Osian begged off a second coffee. He feared his heart might beat out of his chest from the sheer rush of adrenaline.

Buzzing on caffeine, Osian decided to see if Archie was at his mum's place. None of their friends had heard from him since yesterday. *Guilty conscience? Or grieving son and boyfriend?*

He hoped it was the latter.

The walk over to Birdie's old flat helped Osian

clear his head. He ran into Archie on the steps leading up to the building. His friend didn't seem thrilled to see him.

"Morning." Osian refused to allow him to sneak by. "In a hurry?"

Archie slowed his steps, likely realising Osian was too stubborn to not follow. "The police asked me to stop by the station."

"Is Wayne meeting you there?" He didn't know if Archie had hurt either his mum or his boyfriend, but he believed in the wisdom of having a solicitor when the police had questions. "Arch. Tell me you gave him a call."

"He's better things to do with his time than chase after me."

"Does he? If he's your solicitor, I promise you, he doesn't." Osian grabbed his phone to text Wayne. "Archie. Will you slow down? The police can wait."

"You can explain why I'm late for my meeting with them." Archie adjusted his stride slightly, so Osian wasn't speed walking to keep up with him. "I'm sorry."

"For?"

Murdering your boyfriend?

Murdering your mum?

"Running off yesterday."

Ahh.

"No worries." Osian waited for a few seconds, but Archie didn't continue. "Why?"

"I knew you'd have questions." Archie dragged his fingers through his hair roughly, tugging hard on a few strands. "Seems sodding stupid to grumble about Niall cheating on me when he's dead."

Osian watched Archie crumble in front of him. He seemed to shrink in on himself while tears filled his eyes. *Damn it.* "It's all right."

"He was snogging half the company."

"Two people are not half the company." Osian wasn't entirely sure why he'd decided to defend Niall. He hadn't liked what little he knew of the man. "Did you...."

"Kill him?" Archie swiped angrily at the tears in his eyes. "Of course I didn't bloody kill him. Or Mum. I wouldn't. Couldn't. How the hell can you ask me that?"

Someone has to ask you before you get to the police station or you're going to talk your way into a jail cell.

I probably shouldn't be so blunt with my questions.

Osian glanced down at his phone to read the response from Wayne. "Your solicitor's on his way to the police station. He's already at the office. How do people wake up so early in the morning?"

"You worked night shifts."

"By design." Osian had volunteered for the late-night shifts, mostly to keep on the same schedule with Dannel. They'd preferred being able to eat meals and sleep together. "Could Niall have killed your mum?"

"Osian."

"If you think two detective inspectors won't be asking you even worse questions, you've clearly never listened to our podcast." Osian had the occasional nightmare about his own police interrogation. He hoped never to see the inside of one of those rooms again. Haider made a far better friend than an adversary. "Archie?"

"They're dead. Both of them? Is it too much to want this all to have been the worst nightmare ever?" Archie covered his face with his hands. "I've nothing left."

"You have friends, Arch, who love and adore their gentle ginger giant." Osian wrapped his arm around his friend. "Let's get you to the police station. We'll walk slowly to give Wayne time. We're going to get you through this."

Because I don't want to believe you murdered anyone.

It'd break my heart.

Despite walking slowly, they managed to beat Wayne to the station. Some days in London, going on foot was far quicker than driving. Osian kept Archie from heading inside.

"They're waiting."

"They get paid to wait. The entire purpose of their being is to ask questions. It won't hurt the illustrious detective inspectors to be patient." Osian sat on one of the steps leading up to the building. "Can I ask about your mum?"

"Go on." Archie sat awkwardly beside him, legs stretched out to give him more room. "Ask away. I'm done sobbing my eyes out."

"Did she have any enemies?"

"None."

"Someone murdered her, Arch. She had enemies." Osian pointed out. Being stabbed in the back by her own scissors was a highly personal way to kill someone. "It wasn't an accident."

Archie stared out unseeing, silent for several long minutes. "Niall? Obviously. Not that I want to think he's… he was capable of it."

"No one else?"

"She never said. Competition in her industry might be tight, but I'd never imagined any of them capable of murder?" Archie's statement came out more of a question than anything.

"What about her fired assistant?"

"Philippa?" Archie scratched his head, then tried to get his hair back into some semblance of order. "More of a wet noodle than a calculating murderer."

"She'd been fired." Osian had covered a few cases on the podcast of people who'd found being sacked to be the final straw. "It's a motive."

"Mum had exacting standards. She was lovely and sweet. And demanding. She went through a number of assistants. In fact, a couple of the cast had actually worked with her as well." Archie tilted his head back to stare up at the sky. "Going to rain."

"It's London."

"I miss the mountains."

Osian wondered if Archie would be rushing off at the first opportunity. "Do you?"

"Mr Dennis. One of the constables thought they spotted you out here." Detective Inspector Powell stood at the top of the steps. "If you'd come inside?"

"We were—"

"Just waiting for his solicitor." Wayne jogged up to them, slightly out of breath. "Shall we?"

The detective inspector didn't seem overly pleased to see either Wayne or Osian. He didn't take it personally. So far, he'd been a bit of a thorn in their side through two investigations.

Following them into the station, Osian wondered if he could get away with pretending to be Wayne's assistant. Detective Inspector Powell led Wayne and Archie through the door leading into the inner part of the station. Osian was left outside.

"Mind if we have a chat?" Haider motioned for Osian to follow him out a side exit. It led out into a garden the officers used for breaks. "Your friend's in a spot of trouble."

Osian sat on a bench. He was going to be comfortable for whatever Haider's casual interrogation would be. "Is he? Why am I suddenly suspicious of your willingness to share with me?"

Haider paced in front of him before sitting on the bench across from Osian. "Be careful, will you?"

Osian struggled to parse out what the warning meant. *Be careful investigating? Be careful with your potentially murderous friend?* "With what? Overly vigorous tooth brushing? Could you be more specific?"

"Your friend may have murdered two people."

May?

Two?

Which two?

Niall and Howard?

"Only two? Could be worse."

"Osian." Haider leaned forward with his elbows resting on his knees. "We believe Mr Bishop may have murdered Mrs Dennis for discovering his many affairs."

"And Niall?"

"What would you do if someone murdered your mum?" Haider apparently decided Osian's immediately clenched fists were answer enough. "Mr Osman may simply have been in the wrong place at the wrong time."

"And you believe Archie did it?"

"What do you think?"

"I think you've got twenty-four hours to hold him. And Wayne's not a solicitor I'd want to be butting heads with in court or in an interrogation." Osian hadn't made up his mind yet on Archie's guilt or innocence. His heart wanted to believe the latter; besides, Haider didn't need his help. "You're wrong about him."

"Am I?"

I certainly sodding hope so.

And now I've got to try to prove it.

"WHAT HAVE WE LEARNED?" OSIAN HAD CALLED Dannel on the way home, asking if he minded company for tea. Wayne and Roland had shown up an hour later with a massive platter from Nandos with chicken, chips, rice, and more brownies than was probably healthy. "Aside from your brother needs a bib."

"You literally flicked your sauce at me. Git." Roland grabbed a napkin to dab at the mess on his shirt. "Can you get me a damp cloth?"

"Are we ever going to have a meal that isn't at least mildly chaotic?" Wayne caught the tea towel Osian launched at Roland. "What am I thinking? Of course we can't."

"Was Niall murdered because he stumbled on Howard?" Dannel wondered if the medical examiner would be able to determine a close enough time of death to figure out who had died first. "Or vice versa?"

"I've no clue." Wayne held a hand up when they all turned towards him. "You know I can't tell you anything about my client's case. Confidentiality is a thing. Plus I'm waiting to hear from Detective

Inspector Powell on when they want to speak with Archie. I'll let you know what I can afterward."

Osian tapped his fingers against the table. "Why did we invite you?"

"Ossie. Rude." Dannel stared at Osian for a moment. "Right. Sarcasm."

"Edwin."

"Who?" Dannel sat up in bed, trying to process the over-enthusiastic yelling coming from the general direction of the door. "Ossie. How much coffee have you had this morning?"

"Abs and I went for an early morning walk."

"And?"

"Stopped for coffee and chocolate croissants on the way home. Tried a triple shot of espresso in a cherry mocha latte. I brought you one as well." Osian set the cup and a paper bag on the night-stand. "I remembered Edwin."

"Again, I ask, who?"

"The actor who claimed to have gotten injured in the loo at the theatre." Osian sat on the edge of the bed. "Saw Ian on his way out; he said Edwin's returning to rehearsals today."

"And?" Dannel pulled himself up, tucking a pillow behind his back. He grabbed his cup of coffee. "Am I going to be buzzing all afternoon with this?"

"Only put one shot of espresso in yours." Osian collapsed backwards on the bed. "Abs and I figured Edwin has to be behind the ghost."

"Probably."

"And if he is, maybe he's behind the murders."

"What's the motive?" Dannel sipped the coffee and tried to get his brain to wake up. "People don't randomly stab people to death."

"Jack the Ripper?" Osian continued on to name several other serial killers.

Dannel glowered over the rim of his coffee cup. "You know what I meant."

"We've only one way to find out." Osian smiled brightly.

The special smile.

The one Dannel had always loved. It reminded him of all their happy times together. He sighed internally and got out of bed; the smile could not be refused.

Coffee and his chocolate croissant didn't make

for a complete breakfast. They grabbed breakfast burritos from a café down the street before heading to the Evelyn Lavelle. They made one last stop to pick up a couple dozen doughnuts for the actors.

Sweeten them up; maybe they'll be more chatty.

They weren't chatty initially. Hope and Derrick eventually wandered over for a doughnut. They cheered up with the sugary hit.

"Why's everyone so glum?" Osian asked.

"Edwin and Pretty Princess P are back." Hope nodded surreptitiously across the room.

"Hat lady," Osian whispered to Dannel.

Dannel quickly spotted the impressively dressed Philippa in conversation with Ian and his newly hired costume designer. "Wasn't she the assistant fired by Birdie?"

"Ian's frazzled by all the delays and… murders." Derrick's voice dropped to a whisper on the last word. "We're running out of time to get the costumes finished, so he hoped Triple P would help."

"Help?" Hope scoffed. "She's a menace. Swans around all up on herself like she's Evelyn Lavelle reincarnated."

"Desperate measures, I suppose." Dannel

exchanged a glance with Osian. "We should say hello to Ian."

And see what we can figure out from Philippa.

We'll have to track down Edwin as well.

"Do you get the feeling we're in the middle of a penny dreadful where the author hasn't figured out the plot yet?" Osian pulled the doughnut that he'd grabbed in half and offered a part to Dannel.

"Life is always stranger than fiction. The odder things get, the more I'm inclined to believe it's true." Dannel brushed his fingers off on his jeans. They headed across the room towards Ian. "Except for ghosts. Don't believe in them."

"Oh, hello." One of the actors stepped in front of them. "Edwin Tilbury. Were you hoping for an autograph? I usually say no. Perhaps a selfie for the 'gram?"

"For the 'gram?" Dannel mouthed to Osian, who was trying not to laugh. "I'll pass. Do we know you?"

Oh, that was definitely too rude.

Bugger.

"We were hoping you'd tell us about your accident." Osian smoothly covered the awkward moment. Dannel nudged him in thanks, realising this was obviously the actor who'd faked being electrocuted. "Must've been such a traumatic experience. Are you channelling it into your work?"

"Close encounters of a ghostly kind," Dannel interjected. "We're budding paranormal investigators."

We're budding something.

If Ossie doesn't quit snickering under his breath, I'm not going to get through this conversation.

"Are you?" Edwin's smile seemed to grow taut, as if pulled too tightly. Dannel couldn't tell if it was from excitement or concern. "How… interesting."

"Shouldn't actors be more practised at lying?"

Osian choked on a laugh and elbowed Dannel in the side. "He means—well, honestly, I'm sure he meant exactly what he said."

"What?" Dannel glanced at him in confusion. *Oh, right, too blunt.* "I've just heard so much about your skill as an actor."

Walk away.

Walk away now. Let Ossie handle the rest of the conversation. It'll be so much easier for him.

"It wasn't me." Edwin suddenly sounded far less posh and more like he'd grown up around the corner from them. "Harold had the idea for the ghost. I just helped. I'm not tech enough to rig up some of the contraptions."

"You mean Howard, right? Go on," Osian prompted when it became apparent Edwin didn't care about his co-conspirator's name.

"Everyone always says the Evelyn Lavelle is haunted. All the theatre fans flock here to see for themselves." Edwin kept his voice low, eyes darting around as if he expected someone to swoop down on him. "We thought if we made the ghost real, the play would be a massive triumph."

"Did you kill him?"

Edwin reared away from Dannel's pointed question. "What? Me? Why? We were in it together. The loo stunt might not have been our best idea. Had a devil of a time explaining to the coppers why I wasn't hurt in the slightest."

"Did you?" Osian prompted when Edwin became distracted by Ian's laughter behind them.

"Yes." Edwin straightened his shirt fastidiously, brushing the sleeves carefully. "Now, if you'll excuse me, I believe the ensemble is waiting."

They watched Edwin head off to a cluster of actors who'd fallen ravenously onto the doughnuts. Dannel wondered if he was as innocent as he claimed. Had they just been playing the ultimate prank?

Why had someone killed Howard then?

And Niall?

And Birdie?

"Does he realise he's cosplaying as an actor?"

"How meta. The actor is acting as an actor." Dannel grinned at Osian, who seemed equally bemused. "What now? He hasn't really cleared matters up for us. It's more muddied than ever."

Osian looped his arm around Dannel's. "Let's assume the murders are connected. Maybe not all three, but two of them. If so, if we determine the motive for Birdie's, it might lead us to which of the second ones came first. Niall or Howard."

"My bet's on Howard. He set up the prank. He's part of the company, where Niall isn't." Dannel thought it made sense—not that they had any proof.

Osian seemed to consider his thoughts for a moment. "Or, what if Niall murdered Birdie. Howard, being around the theatre constantly, threatened to expose him and ended up at the bottom of the stairs."

"Right, but who killed Niall?"

"Got nothing. The ghost?" Osian shrugged.

"The ghost was Edwin."

"Maybe Edwin killed Niall while trying to save

Howard?" Osian did have a point. "We should've asked him about the cameras."

"Maybe Howard handled them? Edwin didn't seem very tech-savvy." Dannel scratched his head, slipping sideways to avoid walking into a part of the set. "It's a bit far-fetched."

"Fart-fetched." Osian snickered.

"You make one mistake in the middle of a school presentation, and you're never allowed to live it down." Dannel shoved Osian into the thick red curtains bunched to one side of the stage. "Ever."

"Fart. Fetched."

"Are you twelve years old?"

"Some days." Osian took a minute to rein in his amusement.

"Maybe he's lying about it?" Dannel tried to get the conversation back on track.

"Is he capable of being a good liar?" Osian grabbed his hand again, dragging him backstage and out through one of the exits into the passageway. "With the performance he gave us just now?"

"What if it *was* a performance?"

"You honestly think he could pull off acting like such a dismal liar?" Osian glanced over his shoulder at Edwin. "It's a bit hard to believe."

They made their way through the theatre into

the hallway outside the dressing rooms. It was quiet enough with most of the production on stage or elsewhere. Dannel felt as if he'd gone from a wind tunnel into the still calm at the eye of a hurricane.

"How do we prove or disprove any of our theories?" Dannel leant against the wall next to Birdie's old room. "There's no 'x marks the murderer' spot."

For all their camera footage and ideas, none of their theories had panned out to a tangible clue. Killers weren't Hansel and Gretel; they wouldn't find a trail of breadcrumbs. It would've certainly made life easier.

"We ask more questions." Osian brought Dannel out of his thoughts.

"Is that what Haider does? Drive people to distraction with questions until the truth comes out?" Dannel followed Osian inside the room. "Hasn't changed much since the detectives released the scene."

"I'm not courting more bad luck by changing dear old Birdie's sanctuary in the middle of a production. I'm Agatha Daniels. Newly hired costume designer extraordinaire." She waved off their apology for intruding in her space without permission. "Ian explained your investigative skills. Nose around if you must."

"Have you found anything unusual while getting settled?" Osian played with a biscuit tin of buttons, shaking it, much to Dannel's amusement. "Smoking gun, perhaps?"

Instead of answering, Agatha chuckled, then seemed to remember something. She went over to her sewing table and pulled a slip of paper out from a drawer. After a brief hesitation, she handed it to Dannel.

Dannel frowned at the poorly written note, trying to decipher the two sentences. "I know what you did. Meet me in the crypt."

What in the world is the crypt?

"Found it stuffed into the pocket of one of the ruined costumes. Hidden in a ripped fold of the fabric." Agatha pointed to one of the gowns draped across the cutting table. "We're doing our best to salvage what we can. And by we, I mean I'm doing most of the work. Ian's not the best judge of character."

"Philippa giving you trouble?" Osian asked.

While Osian got the dirt on the previously sacked assistant, Dannel inspected the note. It was torn from an almost see-through scrap. *Tracing paper?*

Someone had obviously written their threatening note on something close at hand.

I know what you did. Meet me in the crypt.

"What's the crypt?" Dannel interrupted Agatha's rant about Philippa's inability to do anything but flounce around with heavy sighs. "The crypt?"

"Storage area in the basement." Agatha returned to her conversation with Osian.

Of course, the crypt.

Who saw what? Was this why Howard had gone down the stairs? Was he meeting someone, or had he sent the note? What about Niall? Was Howard threatening Niall? If so, why place a note in Birdie's office?

Brilliant.

We have our first real clue, and it's only led me to have more questions.

"We'll get out of your threads." Osian waved at Agatha and motioned for Dannel to follow him out of the room. He grabbed the paper once they were in the hall. "We should ask the cast if they recognise this chicken scratch."

"Why not check the play poster?" Dannel remembered seeing the poster outside Ian's room.

The entire production had signed it for him. "Maybe we can get an idea there?"

"Why don't I inspect the poster? You're looking frayed at the edge." Osian rested a hand gently on Dannel's shoulder. "Maybe a bit of music and a heavy blanket? Centre yourself?"

Dannel had been so hyper-focused on everything happening at the theatre, he hadn't noticed the strain of so much socialising sneaking up on him. "You sure?"

Osian leaned in for a brief kiss. "Go on. I'll bring something for a late lunch, yeah?"

"I…."

"Don't say sorry." Osian shook his head sharply. "I've got my limits, right? Do you ever blame me for them? When I couldn't do anything but flinch and hide when sirens went off? When helicopters gave me nightmares?"

"Post-traumatic stress," Dannel muttered.

"The strain you live under every day in a world that never bends even a little to accommodate your needs can and does cause post-traumatic stress." Osian managed to be both gently comforting and sternly serious at the same time. "I love you with every fibre of my soul. Love you enough to let you have my last bite of cake. So trust me when I say meeting you halfway on rough days isn't even the slightest bit of a hardship."

Dannel blinked at the sudden emotions bubbling up in him. He didn't have the ability to process them at the moment. "Right. I should go."

"All right, Commander," Osian teased, referring one of their favourite video games. "I'll text you if anything interesting happens."

Putting in his earbuds and blasting the *Hamilton* cast album, Dannel allowed himself to enjoy the walk home. Music, a brisk breeze, and no need for conversation. He was jogging up the stairs into their flat in no time at all.

Dannel kicked off his trainers, fell onto the sofa, and dragged the blanket over him all the way up to his head. "Love you too, Ossie."

NINETEEN
OSIAN

How hard can it be to decipher handwriting?

Some people spend far too much time practising their signature.

Once Dannel had gotten safely away, Osian hunted down the play poster. None of the signatures had immediately jumped out at him. Most seemed overly fancy, making it difficult to match to the block letters of the note.

Is it really a surprise? They probably tried to make their handwriting as different as possible. Never mind how different a signature can be from regular script.

Mine certainly is.

Holding the scrap of paper up, Osian attempted to compare each signature to it. The *M* was the only letter with any sort of flourish. He tried to focus on that in particular.

Not every name had an *m*.

This seems far easier when experts on the telly are solving crimes by comparing handwriting.

"What are you doing?"

Osian closed his fingers around the note, tucking his hand into his pocket before turning around to see Detective Inspector Khan frowning at him. "Hello. Found another body?"

"What are you doing?" he repeated.

"Hunting ghosts." Osian felt guilty about the note burning a hole in his pocket. He did intend to hand over the evidence at some point; just not quite yet. "How about you?"

Haider stepped closer to him. "You'll be pleased to know Archie Dennis has been eliminated as a suspect. Our forensic team discovered DNA at both crime scenes not connected to the victims. Your friend wasn't a match."

"You've got the killer's DNA." Osian stared at him. "Should you be telling me this?"

"I'm hoping it'll deter your voracious curiosity."

"Someone read their word of the day calendar this morning." Osian fingered the note in his pocket. He'd already taken photos of it; those would work for his own investigation. "We found something."

"Of course you did." Haider pinched the bridge of his nose. "What is it?"

"Agatha Daniels found a note in one of the ruined dresses."

"And you've all obviously touched the paper." Haider groaned. He counted to ten under his breath, making Osian snicker. "If you're going to trample around crime scenes, you could at least have the decency to learn how to safely deal with evidence so you're not ruining my case for me."

"I didn't find the bloody paper. It was handed to me." Osian was glad he'd thought to take photos, since Haider was definitely not going to let him see the note again. "And now I'm giving it to you."

"As you always intended."

"Of course." Osian itched to ask more questions. He had a feeling Haider wasn't feeling very chatty. "Never occurred to me to withhold evidence."

"You've already taken photos of it, haven't you?" Haider peered knowingly at him.

"No idea what you're talking about." Osian was the picture of innocence.

"Osian." Haider massaged his forehead for

several seconds. "Maybe stick to ghosts and reporting on crimes? Not investigating them?"

"Have you found a match to the DNA at the crime scene?"

"Osian."

"So, no." Osian smiled winningly at Haider. "Any top suspects?"

"You, if you don't keep your nose out of my case."

"Not very professional of you." Osian ignored the groan from the detective inspector.

With a huff of frustration, Haider stomped away from him. Osian waited until he was out of sight, then went back to inspecting the poster. *These are all blending together. If I have dreams about autographs attacking me, I'm going to be hacked off.*

Wait. Blending. Now there's an idea. What if I use photos of each signature to compare online? There has to be a way to shift one on top of the other to see what the differences are.

Eight snaps later, Osian had a decent close-up of each cluster of signatures on the poster. He didn't know for sure what he'd be able to discover. It didn't hurt to try, though.

Comparing signatures wouldn't hurt anyone, would it?

With the police lurking around the theatre again, Osian decided to head home. Haider would probably chase him off eventually. *I'll check in on rehearsals and make sure Ian's doing all right.*

Not that I'm snooping.

Not me.

Slipping through the door to the backstage area, Osian had to squeeze by boxes of props and a rack of costumes on the right. A crack above his head caught his attention. He threw himself back as a massive light crashed to the floor in a cacophony of sound, broken glass, and metal.

Am I alive?

Yes, of course I am. I'm talking to myself, for crying out loud.

Right. I'm not dead. How hurt am I?

Lying on his back, Osian quickly determined a cut to his forehead, a potential concussion, and a slice to his arm were his only injuries. Of those, the first worried him the most. He didn't recall getting hit on the head.

Someone had to have heard that, right?

I'm not sure I want to stand up without help.

Bugger.

Haider's going to kill me.

"Of course, of course, who else would it sodding be?"

Osian sat up with a pained groan, peering through the blood dripping from the cut on his forehead at an agitated Haider. "Thanks for the concern. I didn't bash myself over the head on purpose. Git."

"Take it easy." Haider crouched down in front of him. "Don't move. We've got paramedics on the way. Can you tell me what happened?"

"Massive light dropped out of the ceiling on me." Osian motioned toward the wreckage behind him. "Someone should dust for fingerprints."

"Osian."

"What? For once, I haven't tampered with your crime scene."

"You *are* the crime scene." Haider held a hand out to stop him from getting up.

"Bit rude."

TWENTY
DANNEL

"Don't panic." Roland's first words when Dannel answered the phone didn't soothe his nerves. "Osian's had an accident. He's okay."

"Don't panic?" Dannel tried to keep his cool. He did. "I'm fine. Calm. Breathing."

"Osian's okay. I swear. Just a few stitches. I'm at the hospital with him," Roland promised. "Wayne's on his way over to pick you up."

"What hospital?"

"He's at the urgent care centre at St Mary's. It was the closest. They've only taken him as a precaution to check on his head injury. Plus the stitches." Roland told him to hold on for a second. Dannel leaned heavily against the back of the sofa, waiting while his brother had a muffled conversation with someone. "He's going to be fine."

"Rolly."

"Wayne should be there in a few minutes. He was already near your flat. Why don't you go downstairs to meet him?" Roland stopped for a second time to speak with someone. "Go on. I'll text you with updates once I've seen your Oz-man."

"Rolly?" Dannel stared at his phone, then dropped it into his pocket. He hunted down his keys, shoved his feet into his trainers, and rushed out of the flat, straight into Myron. "No."

"Son?"

"No time." Dannel started forward, turned back to lock the door, and then barrelled past Myron. He took the stairs four at a time. "Go bother someone else."

Myron followed him all the way out of the building and didn't seem inclined to leave. "What's wrong? Has something happened?"

The absolute last thing Dannel wanted to deal with in a crisis was Myron. Whatever his intentions, it only served to add further tension to the moment. *Why can't he go away?*

"Dannel, sweetheart."

Dannel groaned inwardly when he spotted his

mum, auntie, and uncle coming out of the shop. *Hurry up, Wayne.* "Did Rolly call you?"

"Of course." His mum stepped up, pressing her hands against his cheeks then drawing him into a hug. "Your brother will watch over him until we get to the hospital."

"It's just stitches." Dannel didn't think either he or Osian needed their circus of an extended family showing up to the urgent care centre. "He doesn't want a fuss."

"You don't want a fuss." His mum patted his cheek and stepped back. "We'll be quiet as—"

"Our lot doesn't know how to do quiet." Dannel was relieved to see Wayne's vehicle in the distance. "Honestly. Ossie will be embarrassed if you're all crowding him for a scratch to the head."

"You shouldn't go alone."

Dannel shifted his attention from his mum to Myron. "I won't be alone. Wayne and Roland will be there with us. Plus Osian. It wasn't life-threatening. Rolly would've said."

"Are you coming then?" Wayne lowered the window and got Dannel's attention.

"Hang on." Dannel gestured to the gathered circle of his family.

"They can't all fit in here," Wayne muttered. He

nodded over to the passenger seat. "We're on a bit of a time crunch. I'm supposed to be meeting with a client in an hour."

Dannel opted to hop into the vehicle quickly, giving him time to make an escape before the others realised what was happening. "The sooner we get there, the better."

"You're in for it when they catch up with you." Wayne eased into traffic while Dannel adjusted his seat belt. "Your mum's going to hate me."

"You're in love with her youngest son. Her baby. Treat Rolly right, and you've nothing to worry about." Dannel settled into the seat, tapping his fingers against his knee. He wanted to see Osian. *He's fine. They've said as much. Stop sodding panicking.* "She'll tell me off later."

"Mums usually do." Wayne stopped for a light. He patted Dannel's hand where his fingers still tapped incessantly against his leg. "Osian's fine."

"Fine? Fine. Fine. We keep throwing the word around. He's getting his head stitched up." Dannel crossed his arms to keep from tapping again. "How fine can he be?"

They arrived at the hospital relatively quickly, even with traffic. Dannel rushed inside, leaving Wayne to head off to his meeting. Roland met him at the entrance and led him through to where Osian was being stitched up.

"He's had a lucky escape." Roland kept his voice low to avoid disturbing the nurses. "They didn't find anything when they scanned his noggin."

"Oi. They found my brain," Osian called out.

"You know what I meant." Roland glared over his shoulder at Osian before returning his attention to Dannel. "See? He's all right. Hard-headed prat that he is."

"Isn't empathy a requirement for being a police officer?" Osian ignored the nurse who tutted at him. "It should be."

Standing silently in the corner, Dannel watched the nurse wrap things up. A doctor wandered in a few minutes later. Dannel was too stressed to process what had been said; he barely registered they were on their way out of the hospital several minutes later.

"Earth to Dannel?" Osian nudged him in the side. "Which one of us was whacked in the head?"

"Don't joke." Dannel blinked a few times, making himself focus on the present and not all the possibilities of what might've happened. "We've got to stop investigating on our own."

"Or maybe quit investigating altogether? You're

not the police." Roland led them out to the hospital parking garage. "Come on. I'll get you two home."

"And deal with Mum?" Dannel would pay to not have to fend off their well-meaning family. He had no doubts they'd be smothered with attention and food. "Please?"

Roland fished his keys out of his pocket, pausing to stare at Dannel. "Fine."

They managed to sneak into their flat without anyone noticing. Roland promised to convince their mum to give them some time for Osian to rest. She'd probably hold out for a day at most.

Despite claiming to be okay, Osian sank onto the couch with an air of pure exhaustion. Dannel joined him a second later. He listened while Osian caught him up on what happened after he'd left the theatre.

"Was anyone near you when the light fell?" Dannel stretched his legs out to prop his feet up on the coffee table. Osian twisted around to lie down on the cushions and rest his head on Dannel's thigh. "Everyone was there when I left."

"Pretty sure none of them had gone. Haider was there as well. Didn't see his partner, but I imagine she was there as well." Osian grabbed the blanket off the back of the couch and used it as a cushion for his head. "There are no cameras back-stage to see. I didn't see anyone above when I stopped seeing stars, but I imagine they could've rigged the light to fall. I might just be the unlucky sod who walked through at the right time."

"Something's not right at the Evelyn Lavelle." Dannel had gone into their play at an investigation assuming they'd find a prankster poking fun at Ian. Now they had three murders and someone had dropped a light on Osian. "We know Archie didn't do it."

"Right."

Dannel glanced down to find Osian drifting off to sleep. "Yes, you're going to be so very helpful right now."

"Right."

Leaving Osian to rest, Dannel managed to snag the remote and game controller off the coffee table. He queued up *The Hobbit* and allowed his mind to wander. *How do we figure out who the killer is?*

Without dying ourselves, obviously.

More importantly, how do we convince our mums to not beat down the door to make sure we're okay?

And eating.

Why are mums always so worried about eating?

TWENTY-ONE
OSIAN

Waking up the following morning, Osian regretted doing so almost immediately. His head ached, particularly around the sutures, though sleeping on his back had helped a little. He was definitely going to need a few Paracetamol to get him through the day.

"Dannel? Love?" Osian stretched an arm out, finding nothing but empty sheets. "Hello?"

"Try opening your eyes." Dannel's voice came from the doorway.

Osian forced his eyes open. He sat up slowly in the bed, tucking his pillow behind him for support. "You're up early."

"Our mums showed up at seven."

"Our mums?" Osian didn't know if pain meds

would be sufficient to get him through the morning. "Both of them? Together? Here?"

"I've fobbed them off on my uncle." Dannel came over with a tray. "They made breakfast for us. Some sort of pastry from your mum, and mine made the coffee cake you love."

"With cinnamon swirls and extra crumbles on top?"

"I ate it."

"Bastard." Osian grinned when Dannel handed him a plate containing the obviously uneaten cake and a few breakfast pastries. "I should get a concussion more often. Forget I said that. Terrible plan."

"Haider called, wants you to meet him to give a statement. Ian stopped by after the mums did, worried about you. Rolly showed up as well." Dannel sat on the bed, grabbing one of the pastries for himself. "Turns out you were right. The police think someone set up the lighting to fall. They loosened or removed enough of the screws attaching it to the rigging, it was doomed for failure. One of the techs thought it might've taken a few days to finally drop."

"A few days?" Osian had assumed someone had been up in the rafters watching.

"Also, Rolly 'insists we stop mucking about in a

police investigation.' Direct quote." Dannel sipped his mug of tea. "Bit hard to take him seriously when I remember him wearing Winnie the Pooh slippers for a whole year and refusing any other kind of footwear."

"Remember when he insisted on us calling him Noddy for months?" Osian finished up his pastry and grabbed the coffee cake. He'd saved the best for last. "We should check on Ian. Make sure he's all right."

"You're supposed to be resting today."

Osian gingerly probed around the stitches. The nurse had done a brilliant job. His head was still tender, and his arm had developed some spectacularly coloured bruises. "How taxing can an afternoon at the theatre be?"

"Three murders? A ghost? A light dropping on your head?"

"Details."

The light had definitely been set up to hurt someone. No one could've considered it a harmless prank. A step to either side and Osian would've had a more severe injury to deal with.

What've we got?
Howard, Niall, Birdie.
Me?

The light likely hadn't been intended for him. The killer couldn't have known who the light would fall on, which made Osian question whether they'd believed it would drop instantly. If so, who had the actual target been?

Haider wasn't likely to share his thoughts on the subject. Pity. Osian would've loved to pick the detective's brain.

"If we're going to the theatre, you're going to have to run the gauntlet of our family. I've no doubt the mums are at the shop, keeping an eagle eye out for us." Dannel grabbed the last pastry off the plate. "We need a diversion."

"When has that ever worked?" Osian could think of multiple times as kids when they'd tried to get one over on their parents with limited success. "Disguise?"

"Think they'd notice if Garrus and Nathan Drake snuck out of the building together?"

"Probably." Osian knew his mum, at least, kept up with their cosplay. She had a full photo album with them. "We could try walking out. Maybe they won't be looking."

"It's tragic how terrified of our mums we are."

Osian grinned at him. They snickered together like young teenagers. "Let me get cleaned up."

"I'll help."

"Help?" Osian wiggled his eyebrows suggestively. He chuckled when Dannel frowned at him. "Flirting, love."

"With help in the shower when you're injured?" Dannel asked.

"Never mind." Osian waved his hand. "Just chalk it up to a weird neurotypical thing."

Dannel continued to frown at him before finally getting up and heading toward the en suite. "I'll get the water running. We'll have to be careful to not get your head wet."

Yes, let's not get my head wet.

Don't laugh. He won't understand, and he'll be annoyed about it. Don't laugh.

One of Dannel's greatest frustrations was his inability to grasp certain types of humour. Osian did his best to make sure they could share a laugh. He didn't want to ever leave Dannel out of a joke.

"Don't we have a spare shower cap leftover from the time we built the tub costume?" Osian checked his arm over carefully. He hadn't needed stitches on it, but the bandage on the cut likely needed to be changed. "Let's get Operation: Avoid Mum in gear."

"Worst Bond movie ever."

"Operation: Avoid Mum. She'll have her tea stirred with one sugar and no milk." Osian winked at Dannel who rolled his eyes. "What? Adele can do the theme song."

"I worry about you."

After a quick wash up without a quickie, which Osian found highly disappointing, Dannel helped him get a shirt on without dragging it across his bruised skull and arm. They went into the living room to peer out the windows to check for any sign of their family.

"Pity Chris didn't set up a camera focused on the shop. We could spy on them to time our exit." Osian sat on the window ledge. It wasn't the worst idea he'd had. "Why am I suddenly feeling guilty about sneaking out and not at least telling them I'm all right?"

"Mums."

In the end, they didn't sneak out. Osian decided a better plan was to run in to say hello, then rush off under the excuse of a follow-up at the hospital. A little white lie never hurt anyone.

His mum checked over his injuries. She fussed a bit but finally let him sneak away. He had a feeling she was too busy gossiping with Dannel's mum about Roland's relationship with Wayne.

I wonder if we should warn Rolly about the wedding being planned for them when they're not even engaged.

Nah.

They didn't escape completely, though. Dannel's uncle had insisted on giving them a lift. He didn't seem the least bit surprised when they directed him to the theatre and not the hospital.

"Try not to get yourselves killed, right?" Uncle Danny winked at them. "I'd hate to get stick for bringing you over here to your deaths."

Dannel watched his uncle drive off, shaking his head. "His concern is overwhelming."

Once inside the Evelyn Lavelle, Dannel immediately set up his laptop in the back of the theatre. He planned to focus on trying to match up signatures to the note. Osian found a seat closer to the stage to watch rehearsals; he wasn't alone for long.

Hope slipped into the seat next to Osian. "You'll never guess what's happened since your dance with the chandelier."

"I'm not the phantom." Osian didn't think a stage light qualified for a fancy chandelier. "Are you going to share?"

"Pretty Princess P got herself sacked for a second time." Hope leaned in closer, keeping her voice to a whisper. "She was caught sabotaging a few of the finished costumes."

"Was she?"

"Spilt ink on one of the dresses."

Osian had a flashback to the previously ruined costumes. "Did she?"

"She did." Hope leaned in even closer. She peered around to make sure no one was nearby. "Derrick heard Ian and Agatha say someone claimed to have caught her throwing bottled ink all over one of the completed gowns. She shrieked like a banshee when Ian sacked her. Threatened to ruin his 'silly little play' if it was the last thing she did."

"Mildly dramatic." Osian wondered if the police were aware of the threat.

"We don't call her Pretty Princess P for giggles." Hope shifted back in her seat, waving to several members of the ensemble on stage. "I've got to run, or I won't have time to stretch before dance rehearsals."

Is Pretty Princess P capable of murder? Several thrown tantrums don't equal a serial killer. Would she be a serial killer or a spree killer?

And why would she destroy the gowns after Ian had rehired her?

We should do an entire podcast episode on defining the types of murderers.

Too morbid?

Can you be too morbid with a true crime podcast?

"If you think any harder, smoke's going to pour out of your ears." Dannel dropped into the seat Hope had vacated. "What's happened?"

"Philippa was sacked again. They caught her tossing ink on a gown." Osian kept his retelling succinct. "If she ruined a costume this time, was she the one responsible for the carnage in Birdie's room?"

"She might've seen what the killer did and decided we might accuse the killer—not her," Dannel pointed out. "Or she thought the blame would fall on our pretend ghost."

"Think the police checked the light for fingerprints?"

"What?" Dannel stared at him in confusion at the sudden change of subject.

"Wondering if we can link the phantom moment to either of our suspects." Osian knew neither of the detectives working on the case would volunteer information. "Did Ian say anything?"

"Loads."

"About the case."

"They haven't called the police." Dannel pointed to Ian, who was flitting around on stage.

Osian turned slowly away from the rehearsal. "I'm sorry, what?"

"Ian claimed they'd dealt with the vandalism as a production issue. Agatha argued for contacting the police. Not sure if she's changed his mind yet. We've got no meddling detective inspectors for a while, at least." Dannel got to his feet while Osian processed what he'd said. "They're all still on stage for the short term."

"What could a little poking around hurt?" Osian was grateful when Dannel didn't point out the obvious. "Maybe we can snap a few photos. Try to avoid touching anything. Agatha's clever enough to convince Ian to call the police at some point."

"I found sod all with the signatures," Dannel commented while they left the stalls to head backstage. "Do we know anyone who's clever with handwriting?"

"My mum, according to her careful analysis of my forged teacher's note in sixth form." Osian chuckled along with Dannel. "Never tried that again. What kid doesn't do it at least once? Put your hand down. We're not all exceptionally honest prats."

"Rude."

Osian checked the hallway for stray cast members before heading straight for the costume room. He stopped when Dannel grabbed his shoulder. "What?"

"Gloves." Dannel pulled a box out of his backpack. He tossed a pair to Osian. "Evie grabbed a box for me from the station."

"How very official of us," Osian teased.

"Pillock." Dannel eased on two of the gloves. "Maybe we can keep from buggering up another crime scene with our fingerprints."

Moving into the room, Osian glanced around. Nothing stood out to him at first view. No shredded fabric like the previous time.

"I'm not seeing any ruined costumes." Dannel checked the rack of clothes in the corner. "Maybe in the bin?"

"Never met a costumer who didn't save every possible scrap. Fabric gets expensive." Osian snooped around. He picked up a dry cleaning bag in the corner. "See? I bet she's going to see if they can get any of the ink out."

Despite a thorough inspection, they didn't find any clues. No obvious smoking gun. Dannel had found a note from Agatha obviously meant for

Philippa about a complaint from Edwin over his costume.

"Him again?" Dannel leaned over his shoulder to read the note. "He does keep popping up like a pimple. Think his moaning sent Pretty Princess P over the edge?"

Osian carefully replaced the note on the desk. "Let's leave before we get caught sneaking around with gloves on. Might look a bit suspicious."

"Who caught Philippa in the act?" Dannel asked.

"No idea. Why?" Osian tugged off his gloves, shoving them into his pockets while Dannel did the same.

Dannel gestured down the hall to where Edwin was coming out of the loo, drying his hands on a towel. Even from a distance, they could see the tinge of green on his fingertips. "Maybe Philippa was innocent."

"What are you doing here?"

Osian glanced over his shoulder to find the two inspectors along with Ian at the other end of the hall. He turned back to find Edwin gone. *Bugger.* "Therapy."

"I beg your pardon." Haider caught up with them.

"Making sure I'm not unduly traumatised by the incident." Osian smiled innocently. "Theatre hasn't sent me into a panic yet. Think we're fine. Lovely to see you. Must head home to rest."

To his surprise, they managed to get out of the theatre without the police stopping them. Haider obviously had a crime scene to reinvestigate. Osian grabbed Dannel's hand, leaning his head against his shoulder.

"Tired?"

"A bit," Osian admitted. "We've got to ask Edwin questions."

"We've got to tell the inspectors what we saw."

"Of course."

After we ask our questions.

Unfortunately, Edwin had obviously skipped out of the theatre. They would've seen him before they left, otherwise. Osian messaged Hope to ask her to shoot him a text if the wayward actor reappeared.

"Home?" Dannel asked.

"Definitely." Osian knew they'd already pushed their luck. "Before the police decide to lock us up for our own safety."

TWENTY-TWO

DANNEL

THE FOLLOWING MORNING, DANNEL LEFT OSIAN TO sleep in for a second morning. He'd promised his uncle he'd sweep out the staircases. Given they got such a break on rent, they always tried to help out where possible.

"Hello, sweetheart."

Dannel eased the headphones out of his ears and leaned over the railing to spot his mum below. "Up early."

"Is it a short sentence kind of morning?" She climbed the stairs up to meet him. "Can we chat?"

Dannel leaned his arms on the top of the broom. "About Myron?"

"Always so perceptive." She reached out to pat his arm gently. "Your auntie and I have been baking a few treats for the shop. Want to come down for a quick breakfast while your Ossie sleeps?"

No, I don't.

Dannel knew he couldn't avoid the topic forever. He hated being ambushed early in the morning. "Fine."

"Fine as in you're humouring me because you don't want to say no, or fine as in you're looking forward to sharing breakfast with your loving mum?" She smiled softly at him. "We don't have to chat about your dad."

"Fine." Dannel shrugged.

"Why don't you finish sweeping up first? Give yourself time to decide if you're hungry." His mum patted his hand one last time, then headed down the stairs. "We've got a fresh pot of coffee going as well."

With a barely audible grunt in response, Dannel returned to his sweeping. He made his way quickly from the top floor all the way down to the ground. Ian poked his head out to wave cheerfully and offer a fresh-baked biscuit.

Dannel wrapped up the sweeping and finished the biscuit. He never knew what to expect from family talks. *Might as well get it over with. They'll catch up with me eventually if I don't.*

Maybe I should wake Ossie up.

The ambush didn't start as painfully as Dannel feared. His mum, auntie, uncle, and Myron sat around one of the tables in the corner of the shop, enjoying coffee and cake while chatting cheerfully. He still wanted no part of it.

Most of the time, Roland provided a distraction for their parental types. Dannel appreciated his efforts. He'd hoped the older they got, the less it would be necessary.

Well, over the top with a bayonet.

Maybe I have been playing too much Battlefield.

"Hello, sweetheart. We saved a corner slice for you." His mum gestured to a plate and a mug in front of one of the empty chairs. "Get some coffee in you. You'll be awake in no time at all."

"I'm awake now. Swept the stairs and every-thing." Dannel added an extra sugar cube to his coffee. Osian was the only one who ever made it perfect. "I don't sleepwalk either."

"Not what they meant." Osian stepped up behind Dannel, draping an arm over one shoulder and resting his chin on the other. "Are you having brekkie without me?"

Dannel's stress lowered almost immediately. "There's cake."

"So." Osian paused to grab a large slice of cake. "What's on the secret brekkie committee agenda this morning?"

"Breakfast?" Myriam raised her mug at them. "There's room at the table for you both."

Osian didn't take a seat. He kept Dannel from sitting as well. "Is the brekkie committee ambushing Dannel without warning?"

"Ossie," Dannel muttered. He didn't necessarily disagree with the accusatory nature of the question. They'd had a few conversations over the years with family about not springing things on him. "It might just be breakfast."

"It isn't." Osian sounded utterly confident in his assessment.

"I only want a chance for a chat with my son." Myron chose to break into the conversation, drawing Dannel's attention. "A simple family breakfast."

All of the stress in Dannel broke almost instantly. He'd spent months, years even, trying to maintain peace without expressing his feelings on what had happened. Being ambushed after a stressful day left him without his usual internal buffer.

"You can't force a close relationship. You

swanned off on us. You and Mum decided it was better for Rolly and me to get used to being a family of three. I get adults can grow apart. I understand the decision to divorce now. I'll never grasp how you figured keeping your distance would be good for us." Dannel slammed his hand on the table to stop Myron from interrupting. "All you did was confuse us. Me. You left me feeling as though I'd done something wrong. You made a mistake. People do. I forgive you. But there's no magic wand to wipe away the painful memories of inadequacy. Quit trying to make me fit into your timetable. We'll get there. Eventually."

And with that, Dannel ran out of words. He'd practised telling off his father so many times in his head and in front of the mirror. The verbal tsunami had been brilliant and exhausting.

Now what?

"Lovely to see all of you. We'll just take the cake." Osian stretched an arm out to grab the platter off the table. He caught Dannel's hand and led him out of the shop. "You stunned them into silence. We'll sneak upstairs with our spoils of war."

They made it to their flat without anyone following. Dannel fully expected a family invasion.

Quiet acceptance wasn't in their make-up on a genetic level.

Sinking onto the sofa, Dannel stared up at the ceiling. He heard Osian pottering around in the kitchen. His morning had started out so well.

"Coffee?" Osian held up a mug in front of Dannel.

"What?" Dannel blinked in surprise at the N7 mug hovering near his head. "Sorry."

"Gave you twenty minutes to process but heard your tummy rumbling. Coffee. Cake." Osian handed the mug over, then paused when a knock sounded. "Bugger. We'll ignore them."

"Oi. Open up, you two. Olivia and I want a word," Roland yelled through the door, pounding on it again. "C'mon. It's just us."

Once Dannel nodded, Osian went to let their siblings in. Olivia shoved in by her brother. She lifted up a large sack of muffins, grabbing one and handing the bag to Roland behind her.

"By the by, I warned Mum not to listen to Dad on his plans." Roland rummaged around in their fridge and came out with a bottle of juice. "He mentioned wanting to do a get-together. I said to wait. No one ever listens to me about family gatherings."

"That's because we all remember the time you suggested a joint family vacation. You rented the house. Claimed it was practically a country estate." Osian grabbed the sack of muffins to find a chocolate-cherry one for himself. "And what happened? It was a one-bedroom cottage with a leaky roof and no working loo."

Olivia ignored the squabbling pair and sat next to Dannel on the sofa. "How are you doing?"

"I yelled at my mum." Dannel rubbed at his chest, trying to ease some of the lingering tension. "And Myron."

"You've gotten it off your chest. All those frustrations you bottled up inside. Now, you can heal on your terms." Olivia snagged the muffin out of Roland's hand when he walked by to sit in an armchair. She winked at Dannel, who chuckled. "We've had a word with the parents. They're suitably apologetic for springing it on you."

"She did her disappointed teacher thing." Roland stole the muffin back from Olivia. He handed it back when she glared at him. "Terrifying woman."

"That's my little sister." Osian grinned proudly.

"Right. Enough about the drama. Parents will be parents. They'll sort themselves out." Roland caught the sack of muffins from Osian and got one for himself. "What's going on with your investigation? The one you swore wasn't happening, and I won't mention to the detective inspectors, so I don't wind up on Glastonbury duty."

"Don't fancy trudging around in the mud dealing with drunk partiers?" Osian squashed on the sofa next to Dannel. "We've narrowed our pool of suspects to two."

"Because the other two were murdered," Dannel added. He still didn't know for certain how Howard or Niall figured into Birdie's death.

"Try not to get yourselves murdered in the process." Roland had obviously given up on stopping them from investigating. "And for heaven's sake, don't go alone if you're poking your nose into stuff."

"How's your head?" Olivia asked Osian when it was clear no one had a response to Roland. "Stitches driving you mad yet?"

Osian bent his head forward for her to inspect. "I've got a week maybe before they can come out. Itches like mad, though. Sodding hate stitches."

"Do amateur sleuths get hazard pay?" Roland bit into his muffin and winked at his brother.

"Don't be snarky." Dannel nudged Roland with his foot. "Can we get accident insurance?"

"I loathe all of you. Wankers." Osian feigned a pout while reaching out to snag another muffin from the bag. "Here's what I'd like to know. Do we have one murderer or two? Did Howard or Niall kill Birdie? Or is there another person who did all three?"

"Oz." Roland dropped his head forward into his hands. "Maybe let the detective inspectors figure this out, yeah? It's what they get paid to do."

"Here, look at this." Osian went over to grab the laptop off the table. He showed them the note along with the comparisons they'd made. "I can't tell if there's a similarity or not."

"Have you checked in with Chris? Did his video catch anything interesting?" Olivia ignored the glare Roland sent her way. "What? That you think we had a chance of stopping their curiosity is hilarious."

"Hope springs eternal." Roland sighed.

TWENTY-THREE
OSIAN

"I CAN'T MAKE SENSE OF THIS." OSIAN HAD PRINTED out a copy of the note on tracing paper in an attempt to try fitting the letters over the signatures one at a time. He found it easier than comparing them on his laptop. "Handwriting experts on the telly always make this seem so easy."

Why am I talking to myself out loud? The flat isn't going to answer.

Stepping over to the windows, Osian opened them to let in some fresh air. They'd had a brief reprieve from the stifling summer heat. London had gone through a sweltering heatwave before the rain took the sting out.

Osian leaned out the window, allowing the mild breeze to clear away some of his frustration. He noticed a familiar figure on the street below. "Archie?"

"Can I come up?" Archie tilted his head back and shouted up to Osian.

"Come on." Osian pulled back inside. He glanced around at the chaotic mess their dining room table had turned into. Archie lived in a tent on the side of a mountain half the time. He wasn't going to complain about a few papers strewn about. Dannel, on the other hand, would definitely be whinging about the mess when he returned from working out with Evie.

"Morning." Osian greeted when Archie had jogged up the steps to their flat. "Haven't seen you in a few days."

Archie trudged inside, immediately heading over to sink down on the sofa. He tilted his head against the cushion with a groan. "I thought being cleared would make everything better. Feel like complete rubbish."

"You've had a rough couple of weeks." Osian grabbed a couple beers from the fridge. He handed one to Archie, then went over to grab the copy of the note. "Does this handwriting seem familiar to you? Maybe your mum's or Niall's?"

"Not really." Archie stared at the paper while

clutching the bottle of beer. "You don't have to do this anymore. I'm free and clear. You've already been hurt."

"Exactly. Someone's tried to do me in as well." Osian refused to let the subject rest until they knew who was behind the murders. His curiosity had been piqued. "There's still a killer out there."

And who knows if they're finished.

After three deaths, what if the killer did simply vanish? It would add yet another legend to the darker side history of the West End. The Evelyn Lavelle murders might simply join the London theatre lore.

"Oz?"

Osian glanced over to find Archie watching him in concern. "Sorry. Lost in thought for a mo. You all right?"

"Is it normal to be so angry and devastated at the same time? Feels like my heart was ripped twice with Niall's death." Archie dug a nail into the label on the bottle, peeling it away in ragged strips. "I'm sad about Mum. Losing her has almost been easier, though. Am I a rotten son?"

"She wasn't snogging half the actors and crew at the Evelyn Lavelle."

"Oz."

"Well, she wasn't." Osian sat beside Archie. "Listen, Arch, my point is Niall broke your heart twice."

"Twice?"

"He did. And then, as you're grieving the loss of your mum. You find out the new love in your life was screwing around with a number of other people. And then he dies." Osian figured that would be enough to mess with anyone's head. "Give yourself time to process. You can't make yourself feel better instantly. No matter how hard you try."

"I don't know, Oz." Archie dragged a hand across his face, sighing deeply. "I just don't know what I'm doing."

"Not trying to be rude, but you look as if you haven't slept in ages. Why don't you sneak in a few hours on the pull-out bed in our spare room? You're absolutely knackered." Osian didn't give the gentle ginger giant a chance to argue. "Come on. Sleep will do you a world of good."

"Keep having nightmares at Mum's place. And I wake up expecting her to pop out of the kitchen with a hot chocolate and my favourite flapjacks." Archie downed the rest of his beer and allowed

Osian to guide him down the hall. He barely paused to kick off his trainers before dropping into bed like a felled tree. "I stayed on the mountain too...."

Osian watched Archie drift off to sleep mid-sentence. "Rest up, Arch."

Brilliant.

Grieving ginger sleeping in our spare room.

Prat didn't even answer my question about the note either.

With Archie snoring his head off, Osian returned to his disorganised chaos in the living room. He gathered up the photos of the poster. They'd proven to be nothing other than a source of frustration.

Taking a fresh sheet of paper, Osian jotted down the suspects across the top. *Niall, may he rest in peace—or not, depending on if he killed Birdie. Howard, innocent bystander or double-crossed killer. Philippa, the petty princess. Edwin, bad actor, perhaps figuratively as well as literally.*

My money's on Howard and Edwin. Maybe the two created the ghost of the Evelyn Lavelle together. They might've fallen out over Birdie's death. Could Edwin have caught Howard in the act after Niall's death?

We definitely have to track down Edwin.

How had the police completely ignored him? Motive, probably. There was no apparent reason for either Edwin or Howard to have been involved in the crime. Osian knew from being around the theatre scene that fame could and often did do strange things to people.

Knowing the nature of theatre company gossip, Osian decided to shoot a text to Hope. She'd be able to safely fish for information about Edwin without making him overly suspicious. They might get a chance to get a confession out of him.

If Edwin was guilty.

He sent a text to Dannel as well, to let him know they had a visitor.

On the other hand, they had no way of really knowing for sure about Howard or Niall. *I wonder if Archie has any of Niall's stuff.* They'd travelled together, after all.

After deciding hunting through Archie's bag without permission would be a step too far, Osian turned his attention to cleaning up the mess in the living room. Maybe organised chaos would help him think more clearly. It couldn't hurt.

He stretched out on the sofa after making quick

work of gathering up all the papers and queued up the hours of CCTV footage from the theatre. "Time to watch the dullest reality show on telly."

Maybe he'd see something Chris had missed.

Or maybe he'd take a nap.

TWENTY-FOUR

DANNEL

Sport didn't come naturally to Dannel. His coordination hadn't been brilliant, particularly as a young man. He did find working out almost therapeutic, though.

Running, lifting weights, keeping fit. It had always offered an outlet for him during meltdowns. Evie had been his gym partner for years. She seemed to instinctively know when he needed to run his energy out on a treadmill in silence.

The day after the blowout with his family, Dannel had hovered on the edge of a meltdown. The energy of it almost sizzled under his skin. Evie had come by early in the morning, taken one look at him, and dragged him out to the gym.

Three hours later, Dannel had exhausted

himself of the stress.

"Ready to head home?" Evie came over with a towel draped across her neck. She offered him a bottle of water. "I've got a shift later. And you seem to be feeling better. You pong a bit, though."

"You don't smell of daisies either." Dannel set his weights down and began stretching out his body. "Mum's been awfully quiet today. Not even a text."

Evie wiped her brow with the corner of her towel. "First, you're supposed to be releasing stress, not revisiting the cause. Second, your mum never met a text she didn't like, so enjoy the momentary silence. Third, you dropped a massive heap of truth on your fam. They're going to need time to process as much as you would."

"No fourth?"

"Fourth?" Evie considered him for a moment. "Slowest to shower and change has to pay for coffee."

Dannel watched her bolt for the stairs leading down to where the locker rooms and showers were. "I always end up buying coffee anyway."

Deciding not to rush, Dannel carefully finished stretching out his muscles. He didn't fancy a cramp halfway home. Evie would never let him hear the end of it.

Even with taking his time to stretch, Dannel managed to shower, change, and be outside waiting for Evie. She glared at him while he casually sipped his water. He was unbothered.

"Coffee, then? My treat." Evie caught him by the sleeve, dragging him away from the gym. "Your dad's been hanging around the station."

Dannel caught his toe on the kerb, jolting forward into a jogger trying to sneak past them. He murmured an apology, then glowered at his best friend. "Evie."

"Sorry." She grinned at him. "Think he's getting advice from the chief on how to stop being an absolute wanker."

Dannel stumbled into a lamppost. "I'm sure Ossie would prefer I make it home in one complete, uninjured piece if you can restrain yourself."

"What?" Evie's smile widened even further. She peered at him over the top of her cat-eye shaped glasses. "Sorry. Listen, I think it's doing him some good. He's thinking about his actions. His mistakes. The ones both he and your mum made. You might start seeing a real change in him."

Dannel shrugged.

Evie patted him on the shoulder. "Not saying to

expect miracles. Just give him a chance to show he's willing to change."

"I'll try." Dannel refused to make any promises to anyone. He'd go at his pace or not at all. "I'm starved."

Thankfully, Evie didn't call him out on the sudden change of subject. They joined the queue at Greggs, grabbing coffees and a box of sausage rolls. He got enough to share with Osian plus a number of pain au chocolat for Stanley and Adelle.

"Well, I'm on a double shift tonight. Why don't I drop these off with Adelle while you check on Osian?" Evie shoved him toward the stairs when they got to the building. "Go on before your sausage rolls cool."

Stepping inside their flat, Dannel tossed his keys to the side. Osian was stretched out on the sofa, half asleep with a laptop resting on his stomach. He shut the door quietly to keep from waking him.

"I can hear you tiptoeing."

"I'm not tiptoeing."

"You are. You shush your feet when you tiptoe." Osian sat up slowly with a broad smile. "I smell sausage."

"Isn't that the first sign of a stroke?"

Osian laughed so hard he had to grab the

laptop when it slipped off him. "No. Toast is supposed to be one, but it's more of a myth than anything."

"Want to brainstorm over breakfast? Where's Archie?" Dannel lifted up the coffees in one hand. He headed over to the table to set the drink carrier down along with the Greggs box. "We've got a podcast episode to sort out."

"And a murder to solve." Osian joined him at the table. They sat across from each other with the sausage rolls between them. "Dibs on the pain au chocolat. And Arch decided to head to his mum's place."

"We can share it." Dannel thought, in retrospect, he should've gotten two of the chocolate croissants. "What's this say?"

Osian leaned forward to peer at the barely legible note scribbled on the corner of the page Dannel had been reading. "Not a clue. Elder? Eviscerate? This part further down is a reminder to chat with the Evelyn Lavelle doorman about Howard's ghost."

The doorman at the Evelyn Lavelle had been there for years. He'd notice anything out of the ordinary with his theatre. Dannel grabbed the page from Osian to try to figure out his handwriting.

"Edwin." Dannel finally figured it out. "Or escargot?"

"Why would I write snails in French?"

"You were feeling fancy?" Dannel snickered. He set the paper back on the table. "We'll assume it's Edwin."

"We should see if we can corner him into answering questions." Osian broke the chocolate croissant in half and offered part to Dannel. "Together. No more going on our own."

"Haider will appreciate it." He left out the fact the detective inspector would likely appreciate if they didn't investigate at all. "Did you find anything in the security footage?"

Osian popped the last bite into his mouth, wiping his hands on his jeans. "We didn't get any concrete evidence of murder or paranormal activity. One moment did stand out to me, though. Howard and Edwin having an argument the day before he was murdered."

"Interesting."

"Incredibly interesting." Osian drained the rest of his coffee with a contented sigh. "There's also a flash of someone just out of frame who I think might be Philippa."

Twisting the laptop around, Osian played the

short video several times. Dannel didn't know what made him think the flash of fabric in the corner of the screen was Philippa. It could've been anything, even someone wandering by with a costume over their shoulder.

The clip of Howard and Edwin having an argument was far more intriguing. The two had what appeared to be a heated argument in which the former shoved the latter before storming off. Edwin chased after him, going out of view of the camera.

"Text Ian. See if Edwin's been at the theatre." Dannel wondered if they could corner the actor to get answers. "We have to find out what their argument was about."

"Together."

"You already said that." Dannel sorted through the stacks of notes they'd both made. He found their outline for the upcoming podcast episode. "Did we settle on what story to feature first?"

"The ghost of the Evelyn Lavelle."

"Current or former?" Dannel had a feeling the current ghost wouldn't be nearly as impressive as the supposed haunting of the theatre's namesake. "So, the ghost Evelyn Lavelle."

"An unsolved mysterious death leading to a ghost? Perfect topic."

While Osian continued texting with Ian, Dannel stole the last sausage roll. He stacked their various notes together into some semblance of organisation. They'd made little progress on planning the new episode.

We're going to end up winging it again.

It never goes to plan when we do that.

"Edwin showed up for rehearsals." Osian drew him out of his thoughts. "Why don't you toss your workout gear in the laundry basket? We can chat about our episode while we walk to the theatre."

"Think Haider finally cornered Edwin for a chat?"

"I'm not texting him to find out. He'll yell at us for poking our noses into his investigation again." Osian shoved his phone into his pocket. He fished their podcast notebook out from under the slips of paper and other folders. "We can jot our ideas down if we come up with anything brilliant."

"Too tired to be brilliant." Dannel tossed the remnants of their breakfast in the rubbish bin. "Did Ian have any thoughts about Evelyn Lavelle?"

"The life and times?"

"Her mysterious death." Dannel had been intrigued by the lack of information about how the famed and glamorous actress had died.

Young, talented, and beautiful, Evelyn Lavelle had died under mysterious and suspicious circumstances. She'd been found in her dressing room, collapsed at her vanity while preparing for a performance. No autopsy had been done.

Poison?

Natural causes?

No investigation had been made into her death. The coroner of the time had declared her death a natural one. They had found a few mentions in newspaper columns of a supposed relationship with a high-flying politician.

Mostly in gossip columns of the time.

It made for fascinating reading. They'd have plenty of material to go over in the podcast. A potential old murder mystery combined with a current one at the same theatre.

"Ian found a few old gossip magazines at the theatre. They've got an archive featuring Evelyn Lavelle. We can skim through those." Osian closed his laptop and handed it to Dannel to secure in his backpack. "Ready?"

"Let's try not to get bashed over the head or locked in the loo or poisoned." Dannel glanced around their flat to make sure he hadn't forgotten anything. "Or stabbed with scissors."

TWENTY-FIVE

OSIAN

"Is this why we never did theatre at uni?" Dannel stared at the utter chaos amongst everyone involved in the play. "What's happening?"

"Someone stabbed through the backdrops." Hope sidled up to them. She held out a paper bag of chocolate buttons to them. "Picked these up at the sweet shop around the corner. We all arrived early to find all the beautifully hand-painted scenes had been utterly destroyed."

"Did they find the culprit?" Osian's heart broke for Ian, who'd worked so hard to make everything perfect for his play. "Is there time to repair them?"

"We'll do our best. The whole company is coming together to try to help." Hope offered

Dannel some of the chocolate buttons. "Everyone's going on about the ghost."

"The ghost?"

"Everyone's convinced the murdered spirit of Evelyn Lavelle is haunting the production because Edwin forgot to turn on the ghost light last night." Hope gave a shrug. "We're a superstitious bunch."

Osian gratefully accepted another handful of chocolate. He had a feeling the sugar rush might help him get through the day. "Where's your fearless leader?"

"In his dressing room with a handsome lad wafting smelling salts under his nose." Hope winked at them. "Joking. He's on his mobile being his charming self in an attempt to wrangle an extra week or two before opening night. He won't give up."

That's what I'm afraid of. What if the killer won't stop until the play does? Has this been all about Ian from the beginning?

"Don't worry. We've got bodyguards on him." Hope had obviously caught his expression. "We're not leaving him alone until the ghost, whether human or ethereal, is caught."

While Hope was pulled away by another member of the ensemble, Osian caught Dannel by the hand and slipped through the gathered crowd further into the theatre. He wanted to look at the damaged set for clues. If Ian called the police, they might not have a lot of time to snoop around for clues.

They managed to sneak around to where the ripped hand-painted scenery had been stacked along the walls. Osian knew the set designer had to be completely devastated. He had Dannel keep an eye while he inspected them for clues.

"What are we doing?" Dannel fidgeted beside him. "I mean, honestly, Ossie, what are you expecting to find?"

"A killer," Osian muttered. He crouched next to one of the backdrops. "It seems so easy when we're solving crimes as Sherlock Holmes."

"That's a video game."

Osian couldn't necessarily disagree with his assessment. "Life's basically a video game."

"You should put your words of wisdom on a T-shirt."

"Did you wake up narky?" Osian grinned at Dannel, who rolled his eyes. "Clean cuts. Nothing jagged. Why do this?"

"It's almost as if someone wants to stop the play, but they can't bring themselves to take a drastic enough step. So it's like they're stabbing a hot air balloon with a tiny needle." Dannel paused for a second, checking the doorway behind them. "It might eventually lose all the air. But it won't end as quickly or dramatically as if you took a javelin to it."

"Nothing like a javelin to burst your bubble. If the saboteur and the murderer aren't the same person, the theory makes sense." Osian loved how Dannel brought the world to his level to process. It always led to fascinating conversations. "How many people are running around with long spears?"

"Ossie."

"Wait." Osian grinned at Dannel. "Is a javelin a spear?"

Hope came racing toward them, skidding to a stop and grabbing Dannel's arm to keep from falling over. "We can't find Ian."

"What do you mean, you can't find Ian? I thought you were keeping guard over him," Osian demanded.

"We're not professionals," Hope snapped. "We assumed he'd gone to recover in his dressing room with Edwin."

With Edwin?

Bugger.

"With Edwin?" Osian repeated his question out loud this time.

"Ian was telling him off." Hope barely got her sentence out before Dannel and Osian stormed by her.

They found Ian's space empty, no signs of him or Edwin. Osian grabbed his phone and called their elderly neighbour and friend. No response. He pushed the fear in his belly aside; it was time to focus on what they could do.

"Dannel. Call Roland. Let him know Ian might've been abducted." Osian hung up from his third attempt at contacting Ian. He scrolled through his contacts to find Chris's number. "I'll see if anything's on the CCTV footage."

Hunting through Ian's room, they found nothing useful. Chris claimed the cameras only showed Ian had left the theatre with Edwin. He had no access to any of the CCTV outside the Evelyn Lavelle.

"Do we wait for Rolly or the detectives?" Dannel drew Osian's attention away from his phone. He'd been texting frantically on their group chat. "Ossie?"

"Sorry. I'm putting together a search party." Osian had purposefully kept Roland out of the chat. He might feel the need to involve Haider. "We'll go in pairs. Chis, Archie, Evie, Abs, Olivia, and Drystan all want to join in trying to find Ian. I'll text Haider in a bit to get them searching as well. Just don't want them to try and stop us."

"Why don't I message my auntie and uncle? Or at least Adelle and Stanley. They can take their Thames for a walk and see if there's any sign of Ian. He might've gone home, after all." Dannel eased his phone out of his pocket. "It doesn't explain why he's not answering your calls, though."

Osian motioned for Dannel to follow. "Let's head outside. Anyone in the theatre could be an accomplice at this point. Not sure we want to give our plans away."

They were met at the doors by Hope and Derrick. Osian didn't think they'd get anything by the two dancers. They'd seemed to be the most protective over Ian.

"We'll head to a couple of the other theatres. Maybe someone saw him." Hope kept her voice low. She had an arm through Derrick's. "I'll message you if we find anything out."

Leaving the two members of the ensemble to search the theatres, Dannel used a map of Covent Garden to section off areas and assign them to each pair. His knowledge of search and rescues from one of his firefighting training courses came in handy at times.

"Haider's going to be pissed." Dannel pocketed his phone. "Adelle and Stanley are trying out Thames's skills at a rescue dog."

"In our defence, we have learnt from our past mistakes." Osian wasn't sure the detective inspector would agree with his logic. Haider rarely did. "We aren't going alone."

Knowing the theatre scene as they did, their first stops had been to the series of cafés dotted around the West End. They'd struck out three times before spotting a familiar figure in the corner of a coffee shop. Edwin sat calmly drinking his coffee.

""Where the hell is Ian?" Dannel, as always, got straight to the point. "Did you wreck the theatre this morning?""

"I don't know what you're talking about." Edwin held his hands up in protest. "I never went near the stage while I was at the theatre this morning. Ian's probably off boffing one of his boyfriends."

"Ossie." Dannel put a hand on his shoulder when he started forward. "Let's not get ourselves arrested for causing a scene."

"Did you wreck the backdrops?"

"Of course not, I'm not trying to ruin the play," Edwin insisted. "All we ever wanted to do was draw in more ticket sales."

"You drew in a murderer, you prat." Osian relaxed a little, coming to the realisation Edwin hadn't taken Ian. "Where'd you go after you left?"

"Came here. Bought Ian a coffee. He went off to meet up with someone," Edwin explained. "I confessed to him about being the ghost with Howard. I swear we never touched the costumes."

"The costumes." Osian stared at Edwin. "I forgot about them."

"Yes, the torn costumes."

Osian turned in horror toward Dannel who'd connected the dots as well. "Pretty Princess P. We've chased down the wrong company member."

"Bugger." Dannel scratched his side for a second. "It might not be Philippa."

"Who else is there? Niall's dead. Howard's dead." Osian ticked their suspects off his fingers slowly. "There's Edwin. My gut says it's not him."

"I'm sitting right here," Edwin complained.

Dannel ignored the actor and focused on Osian. "Your gut thought eating a whole pizza plus a lasagne was a brilliant idea."

"In fairness, it was the best pizza ever."

"You lay on the floor of the bathroom, moaning in pain for two hours." Dannel seemed content to ignore the fact that he'd been right there with Osian.

"Well, we were fifteen at the time." Osian decided they should probably focus on their missing friend. He turned back to Edwin. "Are you sure you've no idea where Ian went?"

"None." Edwin shrugged. "Sorry."

"You might want to reach out to the police." Osian trusted Haider, at least, to hear the actor out. They had the killer's DNA, after all, to verify whether Edwin was involved. "Have a chat with them. Take a solicitor. It's always wise to have someone looking out for you."

I trust Haider. The system itself? Not so much.

TWENTY-SIX
DANNEL

"ROLLY WANTS TO KNOW WHERE WE ARE. THEY apparently had a break in the case." Dannel wasn't sure how to respond to his brother's text message. His phone buzzed for a second time; he held it away from his body. "I can't say we're tracking Ian through the West End."

"You know he can't see you, right?" Osian watched him fidget with his phone. "Dannel? Love? Want to head home? We can always leave the search for the professionals."

"Professionals? And a small dog named Thames." Dannel shoved his phone into his pocket, hoping his brother would give up. "I'm fine. Inside voice?"

"Bit loud. I'm sure everyone's glad to hear

you're fine." Osian slipped onto the bench beside him. They'd taken a moment to regroup across from yet another café. Dannel hadn't realised how many there were in London. "Should we try texting Ian again?"

"Why? He hasn't answered the previous twenty times." Dannel jumped when his phone buzzed in his pocket. "Rolly's being persistent."

Deciding to bite the bullet, Dannel checked the six messages from his brother. Each one was more irate than the next. The police had obviously cottoned on to not only Ian being missing but also the vandalism at the theatre and, like Dannel and Osian, put two and two together.

The killer had Ian, likely after tricking him into a meeting.

Or, at least, they all presumed the killer had taken him.

"Do you think the DNA the police found on the victims came from the killer?" Dannel assumed that was the reason the detective inspectors had focused their attention on Niall. Why else had they disregarded Philippa? "If it belonged to someone else, either accidentally or planted there, it might be mucking up their case."

"Mucking up."

"Leave my word alone." Dannel had once spent almost an entire year using the word repeatedly. He liked the way it rolled off the tongue. "Muck."

"I love you." Osian leaned forward to brush his lips against Dannel's, who smiled into the kiss. "And I agree with you. Philippa makes a good suspect. She had a vendetta against Birdie, Ian, and the theatre company as a whole."

"Is she clever enough to realise Edwin and Howard's ghostly prank made the perfect cover?" Dannel appreciated Osian being willing to follow the conversation and not his choice of words. "My theory falls apart when it comes to Niall and Howard."

"Unless one of them was blackmailing her." Osian reminded him of the note they'd found. "Ian probably drew her ire for firing her the second time."

"Didn't Holly say Philippa was obsessed with her image and social media? Check Instagram." Dannel nudged Osian a few times until he grabbed his phone. "Maybe she's shared where she's at."

While Osian snooped around online, Dannel finally texted his brother back. He shared their suspicions about the DNA evidence and Philippa's motives. Roland quite emphatically insisted they quit trying to find Ian.

Try not to get locked in a basement with a murderer.

Funny, baby brother. Hilarious, even.

"One day I will chuck my sodding phone in the Thames." Dannel decided not to turn his mobile off to avoid his brother panicking. He went for one-word answers instead. "Maybe not the river. But I'll turn it off and pretend it doesn't exist."

"And then your entire family will be on our doorstep," Osian pointed out helpfully.

"Wanker."

"Don't blame the messenger." Osian got to his feet and dragged Dannel up off the bench. "Come on. Let's keep going. There's another café on the way to the St Martin's. We can check it and the theatre."

Jogging down the curb, Dannel reached the café first. He peered in through the window at the relatively empty space. No Ian. His anxiety only increased with each second.

Dannel didn't want to consider what might be happening to Ian. "What now?"

"Let's check out St Martin's. Ian's close mates with several members of the production there." Osian led the way down the street and around the corner toward St Martin's. They ran smack into Derrick. He grabbed them both by the arms to keep from falling over. "Easy there."

"Thank god I found you." He stepped back, releasing their arms and taking a moment to catch his breath. "Edwin came by the theatre. He was rambling about being the one to play all the pranks. And then he said you were trying to find Philippa."

Dannel glanced over at Osian. Edwin was either the most brilliant villain in the world, or he genuinely wanted to help find Ian. "Did he have any helpful hints?"

"Not a one." Derrick shifted back and forth, rubbing his hands together before shoving them into his pockets. "I've had an idea."

"Oh?" Osian prompted when he fell silent. "About finding Ian?"

"No. Well, yes." Derrick hesitated for a second time. "I've an idea about where the pretty princess might've gone. She bragged about this fancy studio space someone gifted to her. It's where she claimed to work on all her costumes and gowns."

"If she told everyone about it, maybe Ian went there to speak with her." Dannel knew Ian tended to believe the best in people. Philippa might've been able to convince him to at least talk things out. "Can you tell us where her studio is?"

"I can show you. I've no clue what the address is, but I've a good idea where it's at. A mate of mine lives nearby and saw her going into this studio." Derrick took off at a slow jog. "Hurry."

After a few twists and turns, Derrick led them through an alley between a row of houses and a business. In the back garden of one, a small shed had obviously been converted into a studio. They exchanged confused glances.

"She obviously overstated." Derrick broke the silence. "Should we check?"

"Why all the smoke and mirrors?" Osian muttered to Dannel. "Is it everyone in the theatre world or just the Evelyn Lavelle?"

"What do we do?" Derrick had been trying to peer through the windows while staying behind Dannel and Osian. "Should we knock?"

"We'll take a closer look. Why don't you call the police?" Osian had a good point. Dannel wondered if any of the detectives had been aware of Philippa's hidden space. "Well? Should we rescue the damsel in distress?"

"Sure Ian will appreciate the reference."

"He'll swoon dramatically and want us to carry

him out." Osian inched closer to the shed. "I'm sure he's fine."

Dannel wasn't so sure. "The door won't open with us over here."

"We could always wait for the police."

Dannel stepped around him and reached out to grab the door handle. "Ian might not have time to wait."

Testing the handle, Dannel found it unlocked. He yanked the door open. A thousand possibilities raced through his mind. None of them turned out to be true.

"It's a shed. A literal shed." Dannel poked his head further inside, ducking away from a cobweb. He found an assortment of garden tools. "Ian's definitely not here. I doubt he'd have willingly come in here in any case."

"We've bigger issues." Osian poked him repeatedly in the side. "Dannel."

"What?" He twisted around to find himself staring at a pistol in Derrick's hands. "Where's Ian?"

"Put the gun down." Osian's statement overrode Dannel's question. He angled himself in front of Dannel with his hand out. "Why don't we all sit down in the garden and chat?"

Over the years, they'd both done training courses on dealing with stressful and dangerous situations. Osian, in his previous life as a paramedic, had often talked down angry patients, particularly drunken ones. Dannel could only stand frozen, staring at the weapon.

His mind went blank.

Now was not the ideal moment to lose his ability to process.

Derrick.

Derrick?

He wasn't even on our radar.

TWENTY-SEVEN
OSIAN

Osian wanted to laugh.

There was nothing funny about being held at gunpoint. Dannel shutting down certainly wasn't amusing. Yet, Osian found himself resisting an irrational urge to laugh.

He didn't laugh because of the gun pointed right at him. "Why lead us here?"

"We were going to run the company." Derrick gestured wildly with the gun.

We.

Osian worked hard to keep his breathing calm. "You and Hope?"

Or does he mean Edwin? Hadn't Edwin and Howard been pranking the theatre together as a duo? What was the ghost a decoy for?

"Loveable fool. Pretty and useless," Derrick scoffed. "Hangers on, really. Like most of the theatre crowd. Always hoping for a connection."

"And you're different?"

"Howard and I, we wanted the run of the company. Control of the ensemble and the production." Derrick considered Osian and Dannel for a moment. "I don't expect you to understand. We wanted controlling interest. Ian's a pushover."

"How?" Osian wanted to keep Derrick chatting as long as possible. Someone would surely notice what was happening in their back garden. "You're a dancer."

"Shut up," he snapped. "I'm Derrick Green."

"Who?" Dannel perked up from behind Osian.

From his comment, Osian knew Dannel had gone into a shutdown. He tended to manage one-word answers at best. Osian tried to keep his body between the pistol and Dannel.

While Derrick ranted about his family connections, Osian tried to figure out a way out of the mess. They had to get away from the killer. He wondered if wrestling the weapon out of Derrick's grasp was possible.

Is the safety off?

Doesn't the gun always go off in movies when the hero grabs for it?

"My parents invested heavily into our ensemble and the company when it formed. Howard and Birdie made up the other two main contributors once Ian came on board as director and playwright. It wasn't enough. We couldn't make them listen to my ideas." Derrick's rambling caught his attention. "And Philippa. She made the perfect foil. Sacked and publicly humiliated. She had the obvious motive for murder. With Birdie out of the way, we had complete control."

Not sure that's how theatre companies work.

And what about his parents?

Then again, Haider did say greed was one of the greatest motivators for murder.

"What about Howard? Did you murder him as well? And Niall?" Osian tried to disrupt Derrick's recitation of his non-existent credentials. "Why kill them both?"

"A Shakespearean tragedy almost as brilliantly dramatic as Romeo and Juliet." Derrick adjusted his hand on the gun. "Howard made a mistake."

"Did he?" Osian prompted when Derrick fell silent.

Silence is bad.

We want him talking.

Silence means he's thinking, and I don't trust his thoughts.

"I. Trusted. Him." Derrick ground out the words.

"Did you?"

"With my reputation. With my parents' money. With my heart."

Ahh.

Well, there we go: greed, lust, and a philanderer.

The trifecta of most true crime shows.

"Was he snogging Niall?" Osian eased back ever so slightly when Derrick shoved the gun at him.

"I warned him."

Osian blinked at him. *Warned him? Niall or Howard?* "The note in Birdie's room."

"I saw Niall with Howard. And I warned him to stay away," Derrick insisted. He shifted the gun to his other hand and wiped the sweat from his fingers. "I never did find where the note went."

Given the mess of Birdie's room, Osian could imagine how a threatening note disappeared. It made him wonder if Niall had received it then gone to confront Birdie, assuming she'd been the sender. They might never know the entire truth of the murders at the Evelyn Lavelle.

Part of Osian wanted to tell the still rambling Derrick to be quiet for a minute. The longer he went on, though, the better their chances of survival. *Maybe the bastard will talk himself to death?*

"Oi. Mate. Everything all right over there?" A man leaned out a window a few gardens over, shouting out to them. "I've called the police."

"Why don't you show me where Ian is?" Osian wanted to redirect Derrick's obvious panic, hoping to keep him from shooting them and running off. "You can tell me all about your plans for the theatre."

"Ossie."

Osian couldn't think about Dannel. He wanted to distract Derrick enough in the hopes they'd leave Dannel behind. "You don't have much time if the police are on their way."

"Will you shut up?" Derrick snapped.

Sirens in the distance drew their attention. Osian kept his eye on the gun while planting himself firmly in front of Dannel. One way or another, he had no doubt this would be over soon.

Derrick tugged his sleeve down over his hand, hiding all but the end of the barrel of the gun from view. He motioned for Osian to come closer. "Fine. We'll do it your way. Let's go see the old man."

Osian felt Dannel grip the back of his shirt. "It'll be fine. I promise."

I hope.

As a paramedic, Osian had learnt to never make promises to patients or their family members. It never ended well. He could only do his best with things out of his control.

And a man with a gun was definitely out of his control.

"Ossie."

Osian twisted around. He bent forward to rest his forehead against Dannel's, keeping his voice low. "Text Rolly and Haider. I love you."

"Ossie."

"We'll be fine." Osian didn't get to say anything further. Derrick nudged him in the back with his weapon. "All right. All right."

"If you move, I'll shoot him." Derrick gestured threateningly toward Dannel. "And then I'll kill you. What are two more bodies on my list? Don't move. Don't call the police."

Following Derrick through the alley to a parked vehicle, Osian tried to keep his anxiety at bay while being shoved into the boot. Dannel was safe now. He could figure everything else out.

What if I bust out of the boot in the middle of the street?

Ian was the only thing keeping Osian from acting on his plan. They had no idea where Derrick had sequestered him. If Ian was alive, they might not get a better chance to rescue him.

Plan B.

Easing his phone out of his pocket after waiting for forever to make certain the car wasn't going to stop suddenly, Osian made sure to adjust the sound. He had no idea if Derrick would be able to hear it over traffic sounds. No point in taking an unnecessary risk.

Who to message?

Haider.

A simple message seemed the best option. Osian shifted in the boot, trying to find a slightly less awkward position. He quickly typed a message to Haider.

Osian: Trapped in the boot of Derrick Green's car. Assuming we're on the way to where he's got Ian. Leaving my phone on so you can do your fancy detective tracing thing.

Haider: What were you thinking?

Haider: Never mind. I can list the ways you buggered this up later.

Osian: Alphabetically?

Haider: We're going to track your phone. Do not turn it off. Do not antagonise your abductor.

Osian: I'll be a model prisoner. Is Dannel okay?

Haider: Constable Ortea is with his brother.

Osian: I think we're stopped. Hiding my phone.

Osian had enough time to slip his phone into his pocket and panic about what might happen before Derrick yanked open the boot and ordered him out. "Three stars for the ride. Bit of a cramped seat, but the driving was smooth."

What part of don't antagonise the killer did I miss?

All of it, apparently.

"Let's reunite you with Ian." Derrick managed to sound surprisingly menacing.

And hope to hell he's alive and I can keep us both that way.

TWENTY-EIGHT

DANNEL

ALONE.

Dannel watched Derrick lead Osian away.

Bugger.

Bugger.

The sirens grew closer. Dannel searched for the emergency communication app on his phone. On days when his mind decided spoken words were impossible, he found typing things helped immensely. And the pre-written explanation at the beginning tended to keep everyone else from being confused.

"Sir? Sir. Have you been injured?" A constable approached him cautiously with his partner behind him. "Can we help?"

Dannel tapped the app open on his phone,

holding it out toward the police officers who found him sitting on a brick wall in the garden. The young constable didn't seem to know what to make of him.

Please contact a police officer named Roland Ortea.

Or Detective Inspector Haider Khan.

"Danny?" Roland raced over to him. He'd obviously already been on the way, having shown up moments after the constables. "Are you okay? Were you hurt? Are you in a no-touch mood?"

He typed out Osian's name on his phone and held the screen out toward his brother.

"Detective Inspector Khan looped me into his chat with Osian. They've tracked him via his phone and now on CCTV. They're a few minutes behind the vehicle. He's going to be fine." Roland checked him all over with his hand hovering above Dannel's shoulder. "Were you hurt? You absolutely daft bastard. What were you thinking?"

"Rude git." Dannel was pleased to find two words in his wordless haze.

"You scared me half to death. Be glad Mum's not aware of this little disaster. Heard the call over the radio about some kind of armed hostage situation. And then they mentioned your name." Roland folded his arms across his chest and glared at Dannel. He sighed deeply after a minute of silence. "Why don't I give you a lift home?"

"Ossie," Dannel insisted.

"You need time to decompress. I'll stay with you and take you to wherever Osian is once you're capable of more than one-word answers." Roland had a point despite Dannel wanting to argue.

He didn't have the words to debate with his baby brother.

Sometimes, brain, you're a right pain in the arse.

After a heated text conversation on his mobile, they found a compromise. Roland allowed him to stretch out on the back seat of his vehicle. Dannel popped in his noise-cancelling earbuds and cued up one of his Broadway playlists.

He put *Hamilton* on repeat and tried to get as comfortable as he could in the back of Roland's car. His brother tossed a blanket to him. It was a part of his "help Danny decompress" kit.

Osian's idea. Several of their friends and family had them. It helped when going home wasn't an option.

And Dannel refused to go home.

The heavy blanket and familiar strains of *Hamilton* helped ease some of his stress. It did nothing for his anxiety over Osian's safety. It couldn't.

Nothing but seeing Osian safe and alive could help.

Adjusting the volume of the music, Dannel tried to listen in on the police radio chatter. Roland had thoughtfully turned it down to avoid disturbing him. He couldn't quite make out the words.

"They found Derrick's car. No Osian or Ian." Roland noticed him listening. He adjusted the volume on his radio. "You sure you don't want to go home to wait?"

"Rolly."

"Fine." His brother lifted his hands up in surrender.

"Has anyone told Olivia or his mum and step-dad?" Dannel couldn't imagine Osian's family taking his disappearance well.

"Do you want to be the one to tell Olivia?"

"Aren't you the big and brave police constable?" Dannel stared at his brother, who was shaking his head firmly. "Rolly."

"Olivia is terrifying. Glittery sparkles and terri-fying." Roland held his phone out to Dannel. "You could call her."

"Why don't I text her?" Dannel used Roland's

phone to send the message. His brother could deal with the constant beeping of incoming texts sure to follow. "There. Enjoy the influx of responses."

"Why did I hand you my phone?" Roland carefully placed it on the dashboard, and pointedly ignored the beep. "Rhetorical question. Don't answer."

While Roland dealt with the sudden influx of messages, Dannel leaned against the seat and tried not to think worst-case scenarios. Intense situations were always hard for him. He joked with his brother to deflect from his increasing anxiety.

I should've done more.

Done something.

We could've taken Derrick down. I might've at least tackled the bastard and got the gun off him.

What did I do? Sod all. I stared at Ossie's back and said nothing.

"Danny." Roland broke him out of his spiralling thoughts. "You did everything right."

Dannel stared at his brother.

"I don't need to be a mind reader to see what you're thinking."

"Neurotypicals and your abilities to understand facial expressions." Dannel folded his arms and huffed in annoyance. "And I didn't do anything."

"You're alive. Osian made a decision on the best way to keep you two from getting shot. And now we've got every chance of saving Ian as well." Roland twisted around in the front seat to focus on him. "We'll find them."

Yes, but will we find them alive?

Dannel couldn't voice the question in his head. It would make everything too real for him. "Take us to where they found Derrick's car."

"Danny."

"Whatever they find, I want to be close by." Dannel glared stone-facedly at his brother. He'd find a way to get there by himself if necessary. "Please? Sitting here's going to drive me up the wall."

"One of these days, you're going to get me sacked." Roland settled back into his seat and started the vehicle. "If you two insist on investigating crimes, I'm getting you into self-defence classes as well as scheduling for you two to get private investigator licenses."

"Rolly."

The rest of the drive went by in silence. Roland had apparently decided his point was made. He turned up his radio, listening in to the police chatter. Dannel tried not to hyper-focus on the tinny voices.

"I hate riding in the back seat." Dannel sat forward, resting his arm against the front seat. "It's disorienting."

"Here. Make yourself useful. Answer the messages for me." Roland offered his phone to Dannel when they stopped at a light. "Consider it a distraction."

Driving in London always involved additional stress in Dannel's opinion. He thought they might've made better progress going on public transport or riding a bike. Every second spent in bumper-to-bumper traffic did nothing for his growing anxiety.

Dannel tapped his foot against the floorboard while staring unseeing at a message on his brother's phone. "Olivia wants to know what she can do."

"Tell her we've got it under control."

"Lie."

"Sometimes lying is the kindest thing you can do." Roland glanced sharply to the right when a cabbie cut them off. "Bastard."

Instead of outright lying, Dannel went for a simple answer of "We don't know yet." He signed the message off and tossed the phone on the front passenger seat. They'd resort to calling eventually.

"Danny."

"Don't." Dannel exhaled sharply.

Panic yelled louder in his head than his usual practicality. He didn't have the emotional energy to respond to any more of the messages or answer his own buzzing phone. The drive was going on forever.

Dannel dug his fingers into the palms of his hands, trying to harness his growing panic. "How much longer?"

"We're literally around the corner. I promise." Roland paused briefly. "In fact, I see the detective inspector's vehicle."

His brother eased into a spot between two other patrol cars. Dannel wanted to bolt out of the vehicle, but he had no idea what direction to go. He spotted Haider in the distance, speaking to a uniformed officer.

"Do we wait?" Dannel asked.

"He's seen us." Roland held a hand to stop Dannel from hopping out of the car. "Patience."

"See how patient you feel when it's Wayne who's missing," Dannel muttered.

Haider jogged over to them. He bent down to

Roland's open window, peering into the back seat to see Dannel. "We've found them."

"Alive?" Roland asked when Dannel found the word stuck in his throat. "Ian and Osian?"

"They're down a well."

Dannel blinked a few times. "Down a well?"

TWENTY-NINE
OSIAN

When Derrick forced him out of the boot and stole his phone, Osian had thought a bullet was next on the agenda. Life hadn't flashed before his eyes. Dannel had.

Their life together. He wanted to weep and punch Derrick right in the face. More the latter than the former.

He'd expected to be shot. Staring into the dank abyss of a mid-century well that was behind an old church hadn't been even close to what he'd thought would happen. *I am not ready for this to be some bizarre origin story in my superhero journey.*

They'd definitely travelled further across London than Osian anticipated. He'd obviously been in the boot longer than he thought. *Where are we? I definitely don't remember this church.*

"Get in." Derrick gestured with the pistol.

"I'm sorry. What?" Osian stared between the gun and the well. "Get. In?"

"You heard me perfectly well. Hop in the well. It's not deep enough to kill you." Derrick's assurance didn't make Osian feel better. "Would you rather be shot?"

Are those my only options?

What are my options?

Jump in feet first? Head first? Let the wanker push me into the well? Or attempt a controlled climb on wet stones in the dark?

What could possibly go wrong?

None of the possibilities were brilliant. Going into the well did have the added bonus of not being shot in the head. Osian wished he'd been able to keep his phone.

He placed a hand on the edge of the well. *Slick bricks. Worst rapper in history. Focus on not dying, Osian.*

Taking a deep breath, Osian climbed over the edge of the well. *Thank the building gods someone used rough stone for this well.* He managed to find footholds almost immediately.

Moving down quickly, Osian got his hands out

of the way with a second to spare before Derrick slid a metal grating across the top of the well. *Brilliant. A safety grill. I'm confident it'll do wonders for me.*

"Osian?"

Am I hallucinating?

"Ian?" Osian tried to lower himself to the bottom as quickly and safely as possible. He landed in a puddle of water and had to feel around to find his elderly neighbour. "Of all the wells in the world, you had to walk into mine."

"He made me jump into the well."

Osian knelt beside Ian. His eyes were slowly getting accustomed to the darkness, but he still couldn't make out much. "Where do you hurt?"

"My soul aches." Ian repeatedly coughed, then groaned.

"I can't do triage on your soul, Ian."

"A pity, darling. I'd enjoy watching the attempt." Ian paused for dramatic effect. "The seeing part might be difficult at the moment."

"I'm going to check your body for any breaks."

"Feel me up, darling," Ian encouraged.

With a sigh, Osian did his best to gently check him over. Ian, thankfully, hadn't broken any bones on the way down, aside from potentially a couple of toes. It was difficult to assess in the dark without making things worse.

Despite the summer heat outside, Ian started to shiver. Osian hoped he wasn't going into shock. He didn't really have any options to help Ian from inside a well.

Someone's got to be looking for us by now.

I had my phone on long enough for them to track.

"You've been a lovely neighbour to a lonely old man like myself." Ian continued to shiver beside him. The damp wasn't helping. "You and Dannel."

"Ian." Osian sat beside Ian, trying to provide body heat to keep him warm. "We're going to be rescued."

"I can't go on."

"Ian."

"Do you know how many death scenes I've practised over the years?" He sounded proud of the accomplishment. "Allow me a little pleasure in a dark place."

"Ian." Osian shushed him urgently. "I thought I heard something."

As Ian fell silent, Osian tried to catch any sound beyond the water dripping around them and their own breathing. *There. Footsteps. And muffled voices.* Was it Derrick coming back with an accomplice?

Or had the police tracked the last location on his phone?

"What do we do?" Ian whispered urgently.

"Twenty-million-pound question, isn't it?" Osian kept his voice down. "If we can hear them, maybe they'll be able to hear us?"

Weighing the risks, Osian decided to chance it. He bellowed at the top of his lungs. Ian's hand gripped his tightly.

After a few minutes, Osian heard the sound of the metal safety grill scraping against brick before a little ray of light filtered down. He shielded Ian from the stray bits of stone pelting them from above.

"Mr Garey?"

Osian didn't recognise the voice but from the tone assumed it was a first responder of some sort. "Yes. Ian Barrett's down here with me. He's going to need medical attention. And I'd really like to get out of this sodding well."

In the course of his career as a paramedic, Osian had witnessed a variety of rescues. None had involved a well. He waited patiently, helping secure Ian into the harness to be eased up first.

Ten minutes of careful work by first responders saw both of them safely out of the well. Osian watched over Ian, waiting for the paramedics to arrive. He heard a commotion across the street and caught sight of what appeared to be Dannel and Haider struggling with someone in the hedgerow.

"You stupid git."

Osian glanced over to find Roland storming toward him. "Glad to see you alive as well."

Roland grabbed him in a tight embrace. "What part of don't go running off alone have you failed to understand?"

"We weren't alone. Three of us were together."

"Pity one of you happened to be the killer," Roland pointed out helpfully. "Danny'll be over in a moment. He's trying to feed Derrick his teeth."

THIRTY

DANNEL

Stay in the car.

Stay in the car.

*It's always "stay in the car" when you're the one person-
ally connected.*

Dannel had intended to listen to the request
from both Haider and Roland. He didn't anticipate
catching sight of Derrick. "Why you sneaky
little…."

Across from the church where the first responders were trying to rescue Osian and Ian, Dannel
spotted Derrick hiding behind the hedgerow. *Right.
I've got questions, and he's going to answer them.*

Sliding out of the back seat, Dannel strode
across the street and caught up to Derrick. He
grabbed him by the shirt, swinging him around into

the hedge. There was no way he'd let Derrick get away.

"I—"

Dannel shook Derrick, lifting him off the ground. "What did you do to my Osian, you absolute wanker?"

"Dannel." Haider came jogging across the street toward him with several constables on his heels. "Dannel. You can't kill him."

Dannel turned toward him with his hands still keeping a firm hold on Derrick. "Why would I kill him? I'm not a murderer."

"I—" Haider cut himself off with an impatient wave of his hand. "I wasn't being literal."

"Oh." Dannel hated hyperbolic speech. It always confused him. "He hurt Ossie."

"We're aware. Why don't we let the nice constables place him under arrest? Your Ossie is in the back of an ambulance. I'm sure he'd love your company." Haider guided Derrick toward the two other police officers and then motioned for Dannel to follow him. "Both Osian and Mr Barrett seem relatively uninjured."

"After being thrown in a well?" Dannel didn't believe the detective inspector for a second. He'd been to an incident as a firefighter involving a teenager who'd fallen into a similar hole. "No broken bones?"

Before Haider could respond to his question, Dannel launched into a lengthy list of other queries. His heart started to race the closer to the ambulances they got. He heard a muffled-sounding Ian being his charming self with the paramedics.

"Here." Haider placed a hand on his shoulder, ignoring Dannel's flinch. "He's in this one."

The side door of the ambulance slid open, and one of the paramedics hopped out. Dannel thought he recognised her, but his mind refused to provide a name. She waved him over.

"C'mon then. Let's get you in here to see Oz."

Dannel struggled to get his legs working. "I…."

"I'm Becky. Part of the coalition. Don't worry. I imagine your mind's racing something awful. Oz's fine. We're only checking him over as a precaution." She followed him into the ambulance and slid the door shut, cutting off the sound of Derrick arguing with the constables about how he'd never hurt Ian. "Why don't you have a seat?"

Dannel managed to make it into the seat across from Osian. He grabbed desperately at the hand Osian held out to him. "Had to get your perfect hero origin story, didn't you?"

"Does this make me Bruce Wayne? Being rescued from a well? There was a distinct lack of bats." Osian squeezed his hand tightly. He brought it up to rest his forehead against Dannel's fingers. "I'm all right. A few scratches and bruises. Not going to be rock climbing anytime soon."

"You've never rock climbed a day in your life," Dannel pointed out. He was remembering how to breathe regularly. "How is he really?"

Becky finished checking Osian's blood pressure. "I'd say he's going to have a headache and won't be up for climbing of any kind for the next day or so. We don't even need to take him to the hospital."

"Brilliant. Not sure I want another stay." Osian preferred to avoid hospitals when at all possible.

"Go on. Get out of here. We've got other patients to see." Becky began unhooking all the monitoring equipment from Osian. "My suggestion? Take a Paracetamol and hunker down at your flat with Dannel for a few days."

"Hear that, Danny? No climbing anything. Not even you." Osian got to his feet slowly. He didn't relinquish his hold on Dannel's hand. "Ready to face the wrath of the detective inspector?"

"Hopefully he'll be too busy with Derrick. Wanker." Dannel dragged him into a tight embrace, clutching Osian against him. The paramedics politely focused their attention elsewhere. "I love you. Please, never do that again."

"I promise to never climb into a derelict well ever again." Osian pressed his face against Dannel's neck. "Quit chuckling, you git."

"Will you marry me?" Dannel had thought about it on the drive over.

"Yes, though maybe we can talk it over somewhere other than an ambulance with Becky going all heart eyes over in the corner." Osian tightened his arms around Dannel. "I mean, it's not a bad story to tell in our golden years."

"Why don't you two get out so we can get on with rescuing people who want our help?" Becky prodded Osian in the back. "Send us an invite to the wedding."

They stepped out of the ambulance to find rain beginning to pour down. The second ambulance had already left with Ian. Dannel paused to take in the scene and allow his heart to return to normal.

The rain and the flashing lights from all the emergency vehicles danced merrily against the stained glass windows of the church behind them. Dannel found it mesmerising. He stared for a few seconds before Osian nudged him forward.

"Think we can sneak away without the detective inspector noticing?" Osian nodded toward where Haider appeared to be mid-conversation with two other detectives. "Who drove you here?"

"Rolly." Dannel pointed out his brother standing off to one side of the cluster of detectives. "They'd notice if we stole his car."

"Undoubtedly." Osian leaned into Dannel's side. He wrapped an arm around him to help hold him up. "An Uber maybe?"

"We can't get an Uber from a crime scene." Dannel wanted nothing more than to be home, curled up with Osian and the largest pizza in existence. He knew they had to deal with the police first or they'd be knocking their door down. "Let's get this over with."

Roland stepped around the group of detectives to join them. "Everything and everyone all right?"

"Mostly." Osian frowned when Roland held out a phone. "Not mine."

"Yours is currently in an evidence bag. We found it in Derrick's pocket. You'll have to wait for forensics to finish their work." Roland pushed the phone into Osian's hand. "This one is mine, and you need to call your mum."

By the time they'd dealt with all the calls and a

lecture from Haider about the dangers of amateur investigating, Dannel wanted nothing more than to crawl under the covers. Roland took pity on them, chauffeuring them straight home. He even promised to distract the family.

Adelle and Stanley had swung by on their way to the hospital to sit with Ian and dropped off a platter of sandwiches, crisps, and assorted cakes. Stretching out in bed, Osian and Dannel put on a Twitch stream of a *Mass Effect* playthrough and hid from the world under the duvet together.

"Danny?"

"Yes?" Dannel lifted his head up, brushing crumbs away from his chest. He found Osian watching him intently. "You're not hurt, are you?"

"Genuinely fine. My arms will be screaming in the morning. No jokes about going to the gym." Osian sat up, shoving a pillow behind him for support. "Do you really want to get married?"

"Not mad about the fuss of a wedding. I wouldn't mind getting married, though." Dannel thought an actual proper ceremony sounded like a stressful nightmare in the making. "Want to elope?"

"Can you see my mum and sister handling an elopement well?" Osian shuddered.

"Liv would glitter bomb us until the end of time."

"And glue unicorn horns to our heads while we sleep." Osian lifted his hand up. "Want to put a ring on it?"

"I do."

EPILOGUE

OSIAN

"This is Oz and D. Welcome to this week's episode. We're chatting about one of the grand dames of the West End—the brilliant and beautiful Evelyn Lavelle. Was she murdered?" Osian grinned when Dannel rolled his eyes. "Did she die suddenly of natural causes on opening night?"

"And more importantly, does her ghost still haunt the stage?" Dannel leaned in closer to the microphone. "We spent weeks this summer investigating every nook and cranny of the Evelyn Lavelle Theatre."

We'll leave out the traumatic murders and brief stay in a well.

"For the next few weeks, we'll be sharing details of not only Evelyn Lavelle and her mysterious end, but a whole host of other theatre myths and crimes." Osian slowly turned the page to the next part of their script. "We're starting off with a bang. Not literally."

As Dannel continued with an introduction to Evelyn Lavelle, Osian's thoughts were drawn back to the chaos of the summer. May seemed a century away as opposed to a few months. He'd be glad to see the start of autumn, if only for what might feel like a fresh start.

The past few months since the incident in the well had dragged on unnecessarily slowly. Osian had nightmares of being stuck in a cave or buried alive. He'd begun seeing a therapist a few times a week.

Between chatting with his therapist and talking over a weekly coffee with Haider, Osian felt like his usual self finally. Derrick making a full confession had also helped. None of them had wanted to deal with the extended trauma of a trial.

With the complete confession, Edwin had been cleared of all connection to the murders. He was an annoyance and a prankster. Greedy as well. But he hadn't had any clue about what Howard and Derrick had planned.

Archie had left the country. London seemed to

have soured for their gentle giant. He'd packed up his mum's place, sold everything, and fled for a mountain range far away from his memories.

It was hard to blame him for leaving everything behind.

"Was she murdered? No one seems to know for certain. We found no documentation on an actual cause of death." Osian had found the lack of even a police report strange. "How was an actress, one of the greats of her time, found dead in her dressing room and no investigation done?"

They wrapped up the podcast with the few speculations on the cause of death they'd found in archived newspapers. Dannel wilted into his chair when the recording had been paused. He accepted the beer Osian handed to him with a grin.

"Do you think Ian's play will be a success?" Dannel chugged down half the beer then sat up to help him pack up their microphones. "The theatre community is still buzzing about the murders."

"We'll find out this evening." Osian dug their tickets out from under the podcast episode notes. "He's done a brilliant job of pulling the play together."

Their dapper neighbour had dropped the

tickets off the day before. They'd be attending a preview, with the official opening night the following Friday. Osian was thrilled the play hadn't been cancelled.

It had been a close thing. Ian had spent much of June hiding in his flat. Hope and a few other members of the company had come around in July to drag him to the theatre. They'd all worked hard to recreate costumes and the set.

The kindness of people surprised Osian as much as their cruelty did.

"Why do we have to go so early?" Dannel peered down at the note Ian had left with the tickets. "The play doesn't start until six. We've got to be there at four."

"Tea and cakes?" Osian knew neither of them would turn down a free meal. "Or, knowing Ian, wine and cakes."

"Wine and cake? Olivia will be first in line." Dannel drained the last of his beer. "We've got an hour to get ready."

"Plenty of time for me to help you shower."

"I know how to wash myself." Dannel glared at him. "Inside voice?"

"No, but also, I thought I could *help*."

"Why are you saying 'help' so weirdly?" Dannel stared at him when Osian came closer. "Ossie?"

"We can shower together. You can help me."

"Why… Oh." Dannel laughed when Osian grabbed him by the arm to drag him down the hall. "We have an hour."

"Plenty of time," Osian reiterated with a grin.

Plenty of time turned out to be a stretch. They tumbled out of the bathroom forty-five minutes later. Osian had never gotten dressed so quickly; not brilliant, since Ian had specified dressing up for the occasion.

They scrambled into their nicest trousers and button-up shirts. They tied each other's ties and headed out the door. *Here's hoping this trip to the theatre is far less exciting than our first visit to Ian's rehearsals at the Evelyn Lavelle.*

With autumn not too far away, the weather had thankfully cooled off slightly. The walk to the theatre was perfect. Osian drank in the crowded streets, bright colours, and lighted signs of their little section of London.

They were across the street from the theatre when Dannel grabbed Osian's hand and tugged him away from the crosswalk. *Oh, no. What now?* Dannel paced anxiously in front of him for a few seconds.

"We can go home, love." Osian always wished he could take Dannel's anxiety away or ease it a little for him. "Ian'll understand."

"Everyone else might not." Dannel fidgeted a while longer. "Surprise."

Surprise?

"What?"

"Liv called me. She knows how I hate surprises." Dannel didn't simply hate them; he loathed them with his entire being. "They wanted to plan an engagement party for us."

Osian wasn't even remotely caught off-guard by the news. He'd known this would be an inevitable consequence of his sister finding out. "So, dinner, a party, and a show?"

"Surprise." Dannel brought his hands up and waved them around. They eyed each other, then broke out laughing; Osian leaned against Dannel, trying to hold himself up. "Pretend I didn't tell you."

"I've no doubt Liv assumes you're going to tell me. We're terrible at keeping secrets from each other." Osian couldn't think of a single instance when he'd successfully hidden something from Dannel. "If she makes me wear a unicorn horn, I'm never speaking with her again."

"She did it one time when she was five." Dannel looped his arm around Osian's as they crossed the street toward the theatre. "Better than the time Rolly convinced my mum to dress us both up as Teletubbies for school's fancy dress party."

Osian choked on his laughter. He bent over to rest his hands on his knees for a moment. "I'd forgotten. How are you feeling, Tinky Winky?"

"I hate you. Prat." Dannel glared at him. "We swore a pact to never mention the purple horror ever again."

They found Hope waiting for them just inside the doors. She had her full make-up on but hadn't gotten into her costume yet. Osian was pleased to see her back to her cheery self; the betrayal by her close friend had been hard for her to process.

"How've you been?" Osian asked while she led them down the hall to one of the rooms often used for receptions before or after a play. *Act surprised.* "Where are we off to?"

"I'm brilliant." Hope narrowed her eyes on Osian. "You're a terrible actor."

"Harsh," Osian complained.

Shaking her head at him, Hope opened the

doors, then stepped to the side. Osian tried to muster up a genuinely surprised smile at the crowd waving at him. He appreciated them not shouting out, likely coached by Olivia, who understood how a barrage of sound might overwhelm Dannel.

Unlike other members of their family who often meant well yet failed to see things from Dannel's perspective, Olivia had always gone above and beyond to even the playing field for him. Osian wished everyone was willing to make the effort. He dragged his sister into a tight hug, murmuring his thanks to her.

"Happy 'you're going to get married' party." She reached up to adjust his tie. "I'm so pleased for you both."

While Olivia gave Dannel a quick embrace as well, Osian greeted his mum and stepdad. He was pleased his sister had invited only a small group of their friends and family. Anything larger would've overwhelmed Dannel.

They should both be able to enjoy their engagement party.

"Darling." Ian swanned over with his dressing gown wrapped tightly around him. It flowed like a wispy, silky cloak. "What a joyous event to come at the end of such tragedy."

"How's your toe?" Osian noticed a couple members of the ensemble keeping a close eye on him. "Healed up completely?"

"I'm fine, daring. Better than I ever was." Ian waved his wineglass around grandly. "Have you heard from young Archie?"

"Not a word since he reached his new campsite." Osian had a feeling their gentle giant planned to grieve and heal in silence for a while. "He'll be fine."

Sadness was not a place Ian enjoyed to stay. He broke out into a song of congratulations, drawing in the members of his company littered around the room. It was sweet.

And a bit raucously loud.

The party went on for another hour. The theatre company drifted away to prepare for the preview of opening night. Osian eventually managed to sneak Dannel away from their well-wishers; he led him through the theatre up to one of the private boxes.

Despite having seen so many of the rehearsals, they both enjoyed the play immensely. Ian managed to combine the glamour with a comedic and gossipy telling of the inside workings of the West End. And if there had been a few changes, Osian figured they were definitely for the better.

The interlude came all too quickly. Osian and Dannel stayed in their box. Ian popped by for a visit, bringing champagne and disappearing in a cloud of fabric and laughter.

There had been one bit of the evening Osian had planned for a few weeks. He hoped Dannel didn't hate him for the surprise. It had taken calling in a favour from one of their friends but was definitely worth the effort.

Osian dropped to one knee at the crescendo of the closing act. He held up one of the two rings custom designed for them by a friend who sold jewellery on Etsy; the rings had rosewood bands with titanium cores. "Will you marry me?"

For a brief moment, Dannel stared down at him in confusion. Osian ignored the fluttering of panic in his chest. He wondered if simply showing the rings to him at home would've been a better plan.

Well, too late to worry about it now. Why do I bother with wildly romantic gestures? It never goes to plan when we try.

"I already asked, and you said yes," Dannel pointed out.

"I'm aware. It's only fair I get to propose as well."

"Don't think proposals work like that."

"My knees hurt. Will you say yes?" Osian tried not to burst out laughing in the middle of the dramatic moment of Ian's play. Trust Dannel to be pedantic in the middle of a romantic gesture. "I got rings and everything."

"You can't take back your yes." Dannel grabbed one of the rings. He slid it onto his finger. "Fits."

"I'm not taking back my yes." Osian eased himself up into the seat. "I love you."

"Good. You shouldn't marry someone you don't love." Dannel leaned over for a kiss. "Even if I did propose first."

"Yes, yes you did," Osian readily conceded.

"Good. The rings are brilliant." Dannel nodded firmly. "I love you, Ossie. You're the best friend I've ever had."

***

See what happens next for Osian and Dannel in **book three, *Crown Court Killer*.**

Craving more mysteries? Dahlia has a few for you to be checking out. **Meet Motts and the quirky cast of characters in her world. *Poisoned Primrose* is a quintessential cosy**

British mystery and an all-round fun story to throw yourself into.

You won't want to miss out on reading the *Grasmere Cottage Mystery* trilogy. **With love, wit, and a murder to solve, life for Valor and Bishan is about to get bloomin' complicated in this sweet gay romance.**

ACKNOWLEDGMENTS

Ghost Light Killer was written at the end of 2020. An odd and difficult year for just about everyone, I imagine. I have an amazing group of friends who help me during dark moments, lifting my spirits to help me find some joy in writing. I'm so grateful for every single one of them.

A massive thank you to my brilliant betas who take my first draft and help me turn it into something legible. To Becky and Olivia, who always have faith in me. To all the fantastic people at Hot Tree. And also to my beloved hubby, who keeps me from losing my mind while I'm stressing over word counts.

And, lastly, thank you, readers, for following me on my writing journey. I hope you enjoyed *Ghost Light Killer*. Osian and Dannel are so much fun to write. It was a joy to play in their world for a few months once again.

ABOUT THE AUTHOR

Dahlia Donovan wrote her first romance series after a crazy dream about shifters and damsels in distress. She prefers irreverent humour and unconventional characters. An autistic and occasional hermit, her life wouldn't be complete without her husband and her massive collection of books and video games.

Join Dahlia's newsletter: http://eepurl.com/Q0n0X

Dahlia would love to hear from you directly, too. Please feel free to email her at dahlia@dahliadonovan.com or check out her website dahliadonovan.com for updates.

facebook.com/dahliadonovan

twitter.com/DahliaDonovan

instagram.com/dahliadonovanauthor

bookbub.com/authors/dahlia-donovan

ALSO BY DAHLIA DONOVAN

THE GRASMERE COTTAGE MYSTERY TRILOGY

Dead in the Garden - Dead in the Pond - Dead in the Shop

MOTTS COLD CASE MYSTERY SERIES

Poisoned Primrose - Pierced Peony - Pickled Petunia

LONDON PODCAST MYSTERY SERIES

Cosplay Killer - Ghost Light Killer - Crown Court Killer

STAND-ALONE ROMANCES

After the Scrum - At War With A Broken Heart - Forged in Flood - Found You - One Last Heist - Pure Dumb Luck - Here Comes The Son - All Lathered Up - Not Even A Mouse - The Misguided Confession

THE SIN BIN (COMPLETE SERIES)

The Wanderer - The Caretaker - The Royal Marine - The Botanist - The Unexpected Santa - The Lion Tamer - Haka Ever After

ABOUT THE PUBLISHER

Hot Tree Publishing opened its doors in 2015 with an aspiration to bring quality fiction to the world of readers. With the initial focus on romance and a wide spread of romance subgenres, Hot Tree Publishing has since opened their first imprint, Tangled Tree Publishing, specializing in crime, mystery, suspense, and thriller.

Firmly seated in the industry as a leading editing provider to independent authors and small publishing houses, Hot Tree Publishing is the sister company to Hot Tree Editing, founded in 2012. Having established in-house editing and promotions, plus having a well-respected market presence, Hot Tree Publishing endeavors to be a leader in bringing quality stories to the world of readers.

Interested in discovering more amazing reads brought to you by Hot Tree Publishing? Head over to the website for information:

www.hottreepublishing.com

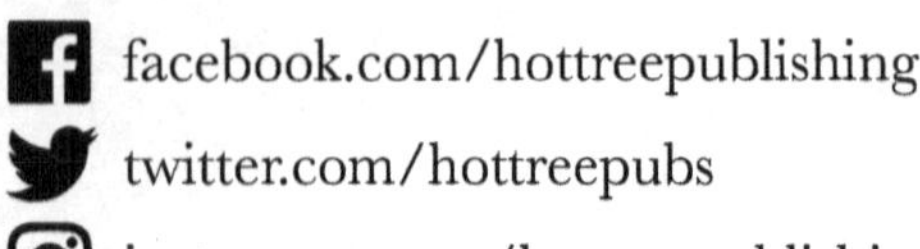

facebook.com/hottreepublishing
twitter.com/hottreepubs
instagram.com/hottreepublishing

www.ingramcontent.com/pod-product-compliance
Lightning Source LLC
Chambersburg PA
CBHW060754190726
48285CB00002B/423